Wishing for the Girl Next Door

Tia Marlee

A Novel Choice Press

Book Cover by Sunset Rose Books

Editing by Lia Huntington

To my husband, my biggest cheerleader.

Contents

Chapter One

Karlee

November

Butterflies swarm in my stomach as I bend down and slip the strappy black heel onto my foot. I've dreamed of this day for years. Exactly what I would wear, what he would say.

Looking at the clock on my nightstand, I take a deep breath and smile. This is it.

A knock sounds from downstairs. He's here.

Slowly, I grab my handbag, and take one last look in the mirror. The off-the-shoulder little black dress fits perfectly, making me feel beautiful and confident. When I get home, everything will have changed. I'll be stepping into the next part of my life.

"Hello, Patrick," I say as my foot hits the last step. "You look handsome."

Patrick looks down at his black suit and gives me a small smile. "Thanks."

He seems off, nervous. My chest feels light knowing he's just as excited about this evening as I am.

"Shall we go?" I ask, slipping into my jacket.

Patrick nods, leading the way out the door and to his car. "You look lovely, Karlee." He says once we're settled inside. "Thanks for agreeing to see me tonight."

I glance at him, puzzled. "Of course, Patrick. I know I've been working a lot lately, but you're still my boyfriend." *For now.* I try not to squeal.

He nods and pulls out of the driveway. The trip to the restaurant is a quiet one. I keep stealing glances at Patrick, but he never takes his eyes off the road. Opening my door, I slip out into the cool November air. "I can't wait to eat here," I say, giving him a huge smile. If he's nervous, he may need some reassurance. Right?

"It's good," he says, and I wonder when he's eaten here before.

I shrug. Maybe he came for a work event.

Patrick opens the door to the steak house, and the aroma makes my mouth water.

"Table for two. Mitchell."

The hostess motions for us to follow her. I slip my hand into Patrick's arm, but he pulls away, placing his hand on the small of my back and allowing me to go first.

"Here we are," the hostess says, placing the menus on the table. "Your server will be right over."

Patrick nods and slides into his chair. I pull my chair out and slip off my jacket, placing it on the backrest. Sitting, I take a moment to look around. The dining room is dimly lit, giving a romantic feel. I want to commit each detail to memory.

"So," Patrick says, putting the menu down and looking at me. "How's work?"

I frown a bit. I hadn't expected to talk about work tonight. "It's good. I think I've almost got enough saved for a nice down payment soon." It's the reason I've been working so hard. So that when Patrick and I get married, we can buy a home right away.

"That's good." He pauses while the server takes our drink order.

"Listen," he says, twisting the stem of his water glass in his fingers. "We should talk."

Suddenly, I'm nervous, and not in the anticipatory way—in the *what is happening right now* way.

"Okay," I say, keeping my voice light, or trying to. "Do you not want to buy a house right away? We can always save the money for when we're ready. I just want to put down roots, feel settled, you know?" I'm rambling, but for some reason I can't stop.

He shakes his head and brings his eyes to mine. For the first time, I see regret where I once saw forever.

"Patrick. You're scaring me," I say, placing my hands in my lap and holding them together tightly.

"I... There's no easy way to say this," he starts. "Karlee, I'm seeing someone else."

"What?" I all but shout, drawing the eye of the other couples in the dining room. "What are you talking about?"

"Please, stay calm," Patrick says, pleading with his eyes for me not to make a scene. "I didn't mean for it to happen. Celine and I, well..."

I throw up my hand. "Stop."

"Karlee, let me explain."

"Explain what?" I whisper harshly. "That my boyfriend and my best friend have been sneaking around behind my back?"

His face turns a bright shade of red.

"No, thank you," I say, standing and grabbing my jacket. "I'll find my own way home."

I storm out of the restaurant, anger fueling every step. I've taken extra shifts. Worked myself to the bone to save for the future. Our future. And he cheats on me. With Celine?

I bump into someone coming out of the door. "Sorry..." My mouth drops open. "You're joking right?"

"I'm so sorry," Celine says, tears slipping down her face. "We didn't mean..."

I push past her before she can say another word. This is not how this night was supposed to go.

June

"I wish you weren't leaving." Mom sighs and follows me to my SUV.

I push the last box into place and close the hatch. "I've already signed the lease and accepted the job. I can't back out now." Sighing, I turn to face her. "I know this is hard. It's hard for me, too. I never expected to be leaving Rockville, but it's time."

I need to get out of this small town and figure out who I am. I've spent the last six years thinking I'd be Mrs. Karlee Mitchell. Those dreams went up in smoke seven months ago.

Mom nods, tears slip down her face. She reaches for me, and I let her envelop me in her strong arms. "Promise you'll call when you get there?"

I squeeze her back. "Of course."

Stepping away, I open the car door, slide inside, and take one last look at the house I've called home my whole life. Tears prick the backs of my eyelids. I won't cry. Not again.

"Karlee," Mom says, wiping a tear from her cheek. "Be safe."

With one last wave, I close the door and start the car. This is it. The day my new life starts.

"Ready, Peanut?" My cat licks her soft brown fur and buries her head into her blanket. "I'll take that as a yes."

I back out of the driveway, and watch in the rearview as the town I grew up in fades in the distance. Thank goodness for audiobooks. Piney Brook is a solid three hours away, making it an ideal location to escape to. I wanted to be close enough to visit with my family, but far enough that I didn't have to face *them* every day.

I tried. It's been seven months since our very public break up. After the first month of anger and tears, I realized I needed to figure out a new path forward. One without men. I started looking for a new job opportunity right after the new year. And Piney Brook General seemed like the perfect place to start over.

I turn up the rom-com I downloaded for this trip. At least romance novels have happily-ever-afters.

No. I won't let myself think like that. Just because Patrick was a dud doesn't mean every man is. I'm sure there are plenty of men who wouldn't cheat on their girlfriend of six years with her best friend. Ha! And to think, I was so certain he'd invited me to the fancy restaurant in town to propose.

Nope, the coward just wanted a public place to drop the bomb that he was in another relationship with Celine. So much for "sisters before misters." We'd been best friends since first grade, and she went and stole my boyfriend.

Apparently, while I'd been working my behind off to save for our future, he'd been starting a life with someone else. How I didn't catch wind of it I'll never know. It's not like our town is huge. You'd think someone, anyone, would have given me a heads up.

Thank goodness I'd been saving all that money. Moving to a new town isn't cheap, but it was easy to put the first, last, and deposit down for my apartment. Of course, I don't own any furniture yet, but it will happen.

The audiobook cuts out and my sister's name pops up on the car display.

"Hey," I say after answering. "How's the fancy new job?"

Keeley laughs. "It's going great. How long till you're in Piney Brook?"

I glance at the clock. "A couple of hours still."

"I'm going to miss you," Keeley says softly. "I'll come visit as soon as this is over." Keels is going into her last year of college, majoring in journalism, and managed to secure an internship at the Rockville Times for the summer.

"Good plan. I should have furniture by then." I chuckle. "Maybe you can bring Scott with you when you visit."

"I can't believe you didn't buy furniture before you moved." Keeley laughs. "I'm sure Scott would love to come. If you have the space."

"I always have space for you, Keels, and that includes that sweet boyfriend of yours." Especially since I know Scott's already asked Mom for permission to marry her. I'm sure by the time they come to visit, there will be a ring on her finger.

"I'm really going to miss you, Karlee."

"I know," I say, reassuring her. "I'm going to miss you too."

We talk for a few more minutes before Keeley's break is over. After saying goodbye, I hit play on the audiobook and lose myself for the next two hours.

I spot a sign announcing Welcome to Piney Brook and turn off the radio. "We're here, Peanut," I say, rolling down the windows to let in the fresh air. I slow my SUV and take in the strip I assume is downtown. A cute diner called Beats and Eats, an elementary school, and a few other little shops dot the main street.

I turn onto Piney Brook Ave. and spot a newer apartment complex off to the left. Turning into the parking area, I pass the pool and clubhouse, complete with a small gym. I am definitely looking forward to the amenities.

Throwing the SUV in park by the front office, I grab my purse and step out of the car. "I'll be right back."

Who knew my best friend would be my cat now? Great.

A few minutes later, I'm standing at the front door of my new apartment. Mine. There's an explosion of butterflies in my chest as I realize I'm finally doing it. I'm living life on my terms. Sliding the key into the slot, I turn it over and swing the door open. "Home sweet home, Peanut."

I step inside, place the pet carrier on the floor, then squat down in front of it and pop open the door. Peanut flies out of the carrier like it launched her from a cannon and starts running around the empty space. Her antics cause me to belly laugh, and, for the first time since the breakup, I feel things might actually be okay. Once she's explored the entire apartment, she settles down.

"Wait here," I say, petting her head. "I'm going to get your dishes and litter box first. We'll get you all set up in no time." She meows and wanders into the space that will be the living room once I find a furniture store. I step out into the hallway and shut the door. Can't risk her running off.

Once I've grabbed her supplies and a few other small things I can carry, I head back up the stairs to my apartment. I grin. I like how it sounds in my head—my apartment.

Opening the door, I move to step inside just as Peanut squeezes through the small gap between the door and my leg and races down the stairs. I drop the things in my hands, and her food bowls clang loudly on the cement landing in front of the door.

"Peanut!" I shout, knowing full well she's not coming back that easily. "Jimminy Crickets! You get back here! Don't you leave me, too, you stinker. You're all I have!" I shout as my foot hits the sidewalk at the bottom of the stairs. "Peanut, come on, sweetie. Don't make me chase you around, please?" I creep closer to where she's sitting by a cluster of bushes licking her paws, stopping before I get too close. I slowly reach out my arm, when right by my ear, I hear—

"Can I help?"

"AHHH!" I scream, startling the cat, who promptly runs up a nearby tree. I slam my hand over my chest where my heart is doing its best to beat right out. "You scared me," I say, turning on my heel to face the offender.

My breath catches in my throat. This man is gorgeous. Dark brown hair that is a bit too long lays over his ears. He's got deep brown eyes like pools of chocolate, and a grin the size of Texas that pops a little dimple out in his left cheek.

"You scared me," I say again. "And now my cat is up a tree." My hands ball into fists on my rounded hips. "Now what am I going to do?"

The man laughs. I feel the heat rise to my cheeks. "This is not funny! She's scared. And now she's stuck in a tree, for goodness' sake."

He schools his face. "You're right. I'm sorry. Evan," he says, extending his hand.

I eye him before shaking his hand quickly. "Karlee."

"Well, Karlee," he says, looking me up and down. "I think I have just the trick. Stay right here."

"As if I'd go anywhere with my cat stuck up a tree," I call as he jogs away. I roll my eyes.

Evan laughs as though this is the funniest thing that's happened all day. He reaches the stairwell, takes the steps two at a time, and slips into the door across the hall from mine. Great, my neighbor is the hottest man I've ever seen, and my cat is up a tree. Wonderful start to this new, no-man-needed life I've set out to build.

"Come on down, Peanut," I beg. "Please?" I'm sure I look like a lunatic out here talking to a tree. I'm dressed in comfortable leggings, an oversized UA of Little Rock shirt, and a pair of sneakers. My hair is in a messy bun on top of my head, and sweat is making the flyaways stick to my face.

Peanut just meows and climbs higher. *Awesome.*

"Here kitty, kitty." Evan's rich voice slides over my ears like warm honey on a biscuit. He shakes a little bag of cat treats. "Be a good girl and come on down now." He opens the bag and places a treat on the ground by the tree.

"That's never going to work," I say, crossing my arms over my chest. He shakes the bag again, never breaking eye contact with me. I look back up at Peanut who's now staring down at us from her perch. "She's too stubborn to be bribed with a little piece of..."

Peanut hops down to a lower limb, rushes to its lowest point, and parkours herself to the ground. It took seconds. "Seriously?" I shake my head and move to grab her.

"Wait," Evan says, catching my arm. He opens my palm and places a few more treats in my hand. "Go slow and show her the food. You don't want to spook her up the tree again."

I sigh and nod. He's right. The last thing I need is to have her run back up the enormous oak tree. Opening my hand so she can see I've got more goodies, I slow my pace and walk calmly toward her. I bend down, placing my hand where she can smell it, but far enough for her to have to come to me. As soon as she takes a nibble of the treats from my palm, I wrap my free arm around her and snatch her up.

"Bad girl running out like that." I rub my face against her head. "You can't do that again," I admonish.

"I'm glad you got her." Evan stands there—treat bag in his hand—smiling. "Mittens did the same thing when I moved in. Turns out, cats don't love new apartments." He shrugs.

"Mittens?" I look at Peanut and grin. "You have a cat named *Mittens*?"

He tilts his head to the side. "Yep. Maybe he and Peanut will be friends, now that Mittens has shared his treats." He shakes the bag again, making Peanut meow with longing.

For the first time since she bolted out the door, I'm laughing. "Thanks for your help, Evan."

"No problem." He glances back upstairs at the mess I left when I dropped everything to chase the cat. "You need some help with your stuff?"

"No, I'm good. Thanks."

He looks to the parking lot where my SUV's clearly loaded down with boxes and laughs. "Let me put these away and grab some shoes. We'll have you unloaded in no time. My mom would never forgive me if I didn't help a new neighbor."

I look down at his bare feet. He ran outside barefoot to help me get my cat down from the tree. I shake my head. Who is this man?

"Okay." I nod, resigning myself to accepting his help. I'm tired from the drive, and I still need to figure out furniture and go to the grocery store. "I'll put Peanut back into her carrier until we're done. Don't want to risk her running off again."

He grins and takes off back up the stairs and into his apartment.

Thirty minutes later, Evan has carried up all the boxes from the car. Insisting I unpack while he does the heavy lifting. I'm not going to complain. The process certainly went a lot faster than I had planned.

"Where's your furniture?" he asks, leaning against the kitchen counter with a bottle of water in his hand. He brought a few over from his apartment and put them in the fridge when he realized I hadn't thought to bring any.

"I don't have any yet," I say, wiping my face with a wet paper towel. "It's on my list."

"Where will you sleep tonight?"

I point to a pile of pillows and blankets I'd crammed into a trash bag when I packed. "I'll make a pallet on the floor. I'm sure I can get something delivered soon."

"Be right back." He doesn't wait for me to respond before he slips out the door. Five minutes later, he's back carrying an air mattress and electric pump. "It's not the best, but it works. I use it when my sister's kids come to stay with me." He shrugs and sets the items on the floor. "You can borrow it."

"I..." I don't know what to say. "Why are you being so nice?" I blurt. I slap my hand over my mouth, feeling the flames of embarrassment lick up my neck and into my face. Patrick would have never thought to offer a stranger an air mattress.

Evan's brows pinch together as if he's trying to figure me out. "I'm being neighborly." He shakes his head. "I'm not sure where you're from, but in Piney Brook, we look out for each other. Especially pretty women who are new to town." He winks.

"Oh," I whisper. "I'm sorry. Usually when people are this helpful, they want something," I say, eyeing him. He does seem like a bit of a flirt.

"Nope," he says, popping the *p*. "I just know I'd want someone to offer my sister something better than the floor if they could. Seriously, it's not a problem." He taps the counter with his hand. "Well, the grocery store is back on Main Street. The best place to grab a quick bite to eat is Beats and Eats. If you need anything else, I'm across the hall."

"Thanks Evan, I appreciate your help today." He nods and walks out the door toward his apartment. I flip the lock into place, turn, and look at my mostly empty apartment. What do I do first?

Chapter Two

Evan

Mittens winds through my feet, smelling my shoes. I'm sure he can smell Karlee's cat on me. "Hey buddy." I lift him into my arms and kick off my sneakers before settling down on the couch. "Do you smell Peanut?" Mittens purrs loudly and rubs his face against mine before breaking free and settling in on the couch beside me. I laugh as he kneads the couch cushion with his black paws.

I reach for the remote and flip on the game.

Karlee. I wonder where she's from. Some place where people only help each other out if they have ulterior motives. If her t-shirt is any sign, she went to school in Little Rock. If she's into big city life, I'm not interested. There may be people in your business in a small town, but we look out for each other. My mom would have invited Karlee to sleep in my bed and put me on the couch if she knew the poor girl didn't have any furniture.

Not my business. There's a fine line for a guy between being neighborly and being creepy. I'm no creeper.

"*Bottom of the ninth, and bases are loaded. Two outs.*" The announcer's voice pulls my attention back to the game. The Outlaws need this win. It's been a rough start to the season. Line drive to first, and he's out. Outlaws lose.

Not their game. Oh well. I head to my room to change. The first Sunday of every month is dinner and game night at my parents' house. I grin as I slip a clean shirt over my head. I may give my parents a hard time about this tradition, but I love it. Well, most of it anyway.

Fifteen minutes later, I'm parked next to my sister's minivan, where she's getting the kids out of their seats. I get out of my truck and go help.

"Uncle Evan!" Brody shouts as I unbuckle his car seat. He's three and looks just like his dad. Blonde hair and green eyes. He gets his excitement from his momma, though.

"Hey bud, you been good for your mom and dad today?" I ruffle his hair before I take him out of the seat and set him on the ground.

"Yep!" He grins and runs towards the front door. Mom must have heard us pull in because she's standing in the doorway, arms wide open to catch Brody when he launches himself at her.

Tracey shakes her head and grabs the diaper bag, Emelia already on her hip. "He's going to hurt someone one of these days."

"Nah." I grin and reach for the bag, taking it from her and closing the door to the van. "Mom's used to it."

I make it inside and set the diaper bag on the chair nestled in the corner near the door. Brody's already tackling Dad on the floor. Emelia claps her hands and wiggles against Tracey until her feet hit the ground, and then she's off, joining in the fun.

"Uncle Evan, I'm winning!" Brody shouts.

"Be careful little dude, you don't want to hurt Grampy. He's old." I laugh and duck when dad throws a pillow at my head.

"Evan, leave your father alone." Mom peeks around the corner, her finger pointed at me like she did when I was a kid.

I salute her and laugh. "Yes, ma'am."

Tracey disappears into the kitchen with Mom, leaving Dad and me on kid duty. I may groan, but I love it. These kids are amazing.

"How's work been?" Dad asks, interrupting my thoughts. He grunts and pushes up from the floor. I'm reminded he's not as young as he once was. "Anything good come through the shop lately?"

He points to the couch and sits, patting the cushion next to him.

"Nah, just the same old stuff." I lean back into the orange and brown flowered couch. I'm sure this couch is older than I am, but it's still as comfortable as ever. "How's retirement?"

"Busy." Dad sighs. "I really thought it would be relaxing, but your mom's got a honey-do list a mile long. I'm thinking she started this list the day we got married and just now got around to giving it to me."

"Mom's always kept you busy," I say. "Brody, be careful. Emelia is smaller than you." I shake my head and grab him by the back of the shirt as he races by. "You can't karate chop your sister."

"Why not?" He pouts. "The Turtles karate chop the bad guys, and Emelia's the bad guy."

"She's too little to be the bad guy," Dad says, his cheeks twitching as if he is holding back a smile. "How about you make her your sidekick? What was that girl's name?"

Brody huffs and crosses his arms. "But I don't want a sidekick."

"I didn't either when I was your age," Tracey calls from the kitchen. "But she's the only sibling you have. Be nice to her."

"What?!" I gasp. "You mean I wasn't always your favorite sibling?" I laugh. I'm her only sibling. Not too hard to win that battle.

"Not by a long shot," she says, poking her head around the corner and smiling. "I wouldn't trade you for the world now, but you were a pain in my behind when you were little."

I shake my head and grab my chest. "You wound me!"

"Well, better get over it," Mom says, walking into the living room wiping her hands on a dishtowel. "Dinner's done."

Once Tracey washes the kids' hands, and everyone's settled at the table, I bow my head and Dad says grace. When he's about done, I lean forward to sneak a breadstick.

"Ouch!" I snatch my hand back from the serving tray, rubbing the sting from mom's sharp slap away.

"Evan Christopher. You know better," Mom admonishes, shaking her head and glaring at me. "No wonder you don't have a girlfriend."

Dad chuckles. "Leave the boy alone, Marge."

"Well, I'm just saying," she mutters as she passes Dad the tray of lasagna. "How can I rest knowing my son is all alone? Ever since Louise, you've been closed off."

"I'm an adult, ma. I've got friends. Besides, just because I haven't brought anyone home for dinner doesn't mean I haven't dated." I load my plate up with lasagna and two breadsticks.

"Oh, really?" Tracey asks, between blowing on Emelia's food. "Why don't I ever hear about these dates?"

"Not you, too. Maybe because no one has ever caught my attention long enough to tell you about them." A flash of Karlee crosses my mind—hair a mess and frantic that her cat had climbed up the tree—and I smile.

"Ah!" Mom shouts, pointing at me. "You're smiling the smile! Who is she?"

I laugh. "Mom, I promise, if I meet *the one*, you'll know." I point to my plate. "Can I eat in peace now?"

Mom pouts and nods. Thankfully, attention turns to Tracey and talk of Lawrence's latest business trip to California, and the focus stays off me for the rest of the meal.

By the time seven o'clock rolls around, I'm ready to leave. When Tracey packs the kids up, I take that as my cue and offer to help her get them in the car.

"I've got it," I say, grabbing the diaper bag off the chair and slinging it over my shoulder. I gently lift Brody off of Dad's shoulder where he's fallen asleep, and motion for Tracey to lead the way.

At the door, I kiss my mom's cheek.

"Don't wait too long to find her," Mom whispers. "A life spent with the one you love is far better than one spent alone."

I nod. "I know, but I'm not that old, Mom. Lots of guys aren't married at twenty-six."

She smiles sadly and pats my face. "Drive safe."

I nod and head to the minivan where Tracey is waiting to buckle Brody in.

"Thanks," she whispers after I place him in his seat.

"Do you need help to get them inside the house? I can follow you."

She shakes her head. "Nah, I'm good. Thanks, though." She slides the van door closed and turns to face me. "Let's meet up soon. You can tell me about whoever had you smiling like a loon at dinner."

I blush. "I was not smiling like a loon," I say. "Seriously, there's no one."

"I don't believe you." She pushes up to her tiptoes and kisses my cheek. "But I'm going to let it go because I think you do believe that."

I watch her walk around and climb into the driver's seat. Why they opted for such a big vehicle for only two kids, I'll never know.

I wave as she pulls out of the drive. I love these dinners with my family, but I always leave tired.

"Hey." I smile and wave at Karlee as she comes up the stairs. She's dressed in dark blue scrubs, her hair pulled in a high tight ponytail. "Coming home from the night shift, or forgetting something?"

It's been a week since she moved in, and I haven't seen any furniture deliveries. Of course, they could have come while I was at work, I suppose.

"Coming home." She pulls herself up the last two stairs by the banister. "Long night." She yawns and reaches up to pull on her ponytail.

I really look at her and notice the bags under her eyes. "Have you been able to get a bed ordered at least?"

She laughs and leans against her door frame. "Nope, I ordered a bed set and a couch yesterday, but it seems they're booked for delivery until the weekend." She covers another enormous yawn with her hand. "The air mattress has been a lifesaver. Do you need it back yet?"

I shake my head no and pause with my keys in my hand. "Listen," I say, working my house key off the ring. "Why don't you sleep in my bed while I'm at work today? I just changed the sheets last night. They're clean."

She is shaking her head no, but I hand her the key, anyway. "You don't have to, but the offer stands. Mittens is a sweetheart, but he may want to cuddle. You could bring Peanut over with you if you'd like. Mittens usually likes other cats."

"I couldn't possibly intrude."

She stretches her arms above her head, giving me the smallest peek of her stomach. My mouth goes dry, but I do my best to refocus. "You're not intruding. I won't even be home. When you wake up, call the furniture store and let them know you found someone who will help you pick up your stuff today."

"Really?" She grins.

She looks energized by the idea of getting her furniture. That makes me happy. "Really. I'll be home by 5:30. What time do they close?"

"I think they close at nine, but I'll double check. Thanks, Evan!" She bounces on her toes and squeals. "Finally, a good night's, or day's, rest!"

"Seriously, consider using my bed today. You'll sleep better." I walk down the stairs before she can argue. "Oh, and Karlee? You're beautiful when you smile."

I don't dare turn around to see her face. Who am I right now? I shake my head and vow to keep my compliments to myself. She's my neighbor. I don't want her to think I'm looking for something from her besides friendly banter in the hallway. Especially when she already thinks people are only out to use each other.

I spend the rest of the day remembering what that sliver of stomach looked like, and reminding myself that neighbors are not for dating. I've made more than one silly mistake today because I'm daydreaming about her, including attempting to put an air filter in backwards. Daniel probably won't ever let me live that one down.

Mom's advice keeps flowing through my thoughts. Am I really closed off?

"Quitting time, guys," Brant calls from his office.

"Thank goodness," I say, wiping my hands on a towel. "I've got plans tonight. Don't want to be late." I wink and waggle my eyebrows suggestively. I think it's hysterical to give Daniel a hard time. Especially since he refuses to ask out the beauty from Brant's wedding.

"The only plan you have is to get takeout and watch TV," Daniel says, tossing his head back and laughing.

"Yeah, yeah." I grin. I love the laid-back atmosphere of the shop. Daniel and Brant are great guys, and they are my good friends. "Actually, I told my neighbor I'd help her pick up her new couch tonight."

"The new neighbor?" asks Brant. "Should we make extra food this weekend?"

"It's not like that," I say, closing the last drawer of my toolbox. "I'm just being friendly."

"So, you're not going to invite her to the cookout this weekend?" Brant crosses his arms and leans into the wall. "Because we would certainly be all right with it if you did."

"I told you, I'm not bringing anyone around unless they're sticking," I say, already wondering if she'd say yes. "I'm sure she has friends of her own, and her own life. I'm just helping her out." Actually, come to think of it, I'm not sure how far away she is from her hometown. She may not have many close friends in Piney Brook yet.

"If you say so," Brant pushes off the wall and heads to the door.

I shake my head and walk out to my truck. Don't want to be late and cause Karlee another night on the air mattress.

I pull into the parking space in front of the apartment building and turn off the truck. For some reason I can't explain, I really hope she took me up on the offer to sleep in my bed. I can't imagine sleeping on an air mattress for a full week. Add in working nights, and she must be exhausted.

Taking the steps two at a time, I hit the landing just as Karlee opens my front door.

Chapter Three

Karlee

"Please don't run out," I say to Mittens as I back slowly out Evan's door. I tried to resist, but the idea of sleep in an actual bed won out. Too many nights on the air mattress have made my back stiff. I was grateful when I got up from Evan's bed and didn't feel the same creaks and groans I've been feeling all week.

"I'm glad to see you gave in," a deep voice says from right behind me. I shriek and jump in the air, slapping my hands over my heart.

"Jeez, Evan," I say, turning to face him. "You scared the daylights out of me, again!" My heart is still racing like I've been through one of those haunted houses at Halloween. "What were you doing sneaking up on me like that?"

"I'm sorry." He holds his hands up in surrender and looks down at his feet. "I'm surprised you didn't hear me with these steel-toed boots on. They're a little noisy coming up the stairs. I didn't mean to scare you. I told you I'd be back around now."

I look at the fitness watch on my arm. He's right; it's already 5:30. "Shoot." I look at him and shake my head. "I overslept and haven't made the call to the furniture store yet."

He grins and moves to open his door. "You're fine. I need to shower and change real quick, anyway. Have you eaten?"

I shake my head. I finally gave up around ten and went next door to climb in his bed. I must have fallen asleep pretty quickly nestled into his hunter green sheets that smell like baby powder and something woodsy that must be all Evan. It surprised me how clean his room is for being a bachelor pad.

"Good, we'll grab a bite from Beats and Eats on the way. I'm assuming your furniture is at the Furniture Barn in Piney Ridge?"

I nod. "That sounds good. Just knock on my door when you're ready. I'll call and verify the hours now." I pass him the key he gave me this morning. "Thanks Evan, I needed that."

Evan nods and slips into his apartment, the door closing with a soft snick.

Peanut meows loudly when I open the apartment door. She's sitting on top of the counter, staring at the door. I sure hope she doesn't do this all night while I am at work. I scoop her off the counter and head to the cupboard to grab her food.

"I'm off tonight, sweet girl, and I'm getting us an actual bed." Filling her food dish, I check her water before giving her a rub and putting her down. I look down at the old t-shirt and running shorts I have on and head to the bedroom to change out of my sleep wear. I'd have been mortified if Evan had caught me sneaking out of his apartment in some frilly lingerie. Even if he gave me the key and permission to sleep in his bed.

I slide on some clean cut-off shorts and a tank top. It's surprisingly hot in Piney Brook in the summer. I'd thought moving a few hours north-west of Rockville would have been at least a little cooler. Nope. Still the same summer heat.

I grab my cell and dial the number from the Furniture Barn card. The phone rings several times before someone finally answers. "Furniture Barn, Freddy speaking. How can I help you?"

"Hi, Freddy, it's Karlee Richards. I purchased some furniture there yesterday. I'd scheduled a delivery, but a friend has offered to help me pick it up tonight if you'll be open."

It feels weird to call Evan a friend since I haven't known him that long, but he certainly has been friendly since I moved in. Besides Mona and a few other people at the hospital, I haven't had time to meet anyone yet.

"All right Karlee, I see your order. We'll be here until nine, not a minute after." He makes a spitting sound, reminding me of the men back home who dip. I've never understood the appeal.

"Thank you so much. We'll be there."

I hang up the phone and do a happy dance. "We're getting furniture!" I scoop Peanut up from where she's busy trying to eat and spin her around. I'm about to set her back on the ground when there's a knock at the door.

"Karlee, it's Evan. Are you ready?"

I put Peanut down and wipe my hands on my shorts before grabbing my purse and opening the door. "Yep, let's go. Freddy said they'll be there until nine and not a minute after," I say, mimicking Freddy's deep voice.

Evan laughs. "That should work perfectly. We can swing by Beats and Eats for a to-go order and eat in the truck if you're all right with that? I'd rather avoid the gossip of eating in."

Evan holds the door open so I can step through. "Sounds good to me. Want me to call it in?"

"Sure, that would be great. I'll take a burger with everything, and fries. A large Coke, too."

I nod and grab my phone to search for the number.

Thirty minutes later, we are in Evan's truck—burgers in hand—headed out of town to Piney Ridge. I take a bite and moan. "This is the best burger I've had in a long time." I lick my lips, grabbing the bit of mayo and mustard that dribbled out when I took a bite. I didn't realize how hungry I was.

Evan chokes on his drink. "I'm glad." He manages between coughs. "So, what brought you to Piney Brook?" he asks once he finally clears his throat.

I consider how much I want to share while I finish chewing. "Well, long story short, I wanted a fresh start and Piney Brook General had an opening."

He glances at me from the driver's seat. "Okay. And the long version?"

I shrug. "You don't want to hear about that."

"I beg to differ," he says before pulling off into a clearing on the side of the road. "Easier to eat if I'm not driving," he says, taking in my confused look. "This burger is too messy." He points to the to-go container where lettuce and drippings of mustard are all over the fries.

"I see that." I laugh and grab a mustard-covered fry. "A delicious mess, though."

Evan stares at me, making me feel self-conscious. Patrick hated it when I took food off his plate, but it's a habit I haven't been able to break. "Sorry, I should have asked before I grabbed a fry."

"I don't care about that," he says flippantly. "Who eats french fries with mustard on them?" He cringes.

I laugh. "Don't knock it until you try it," I say, relieved I didn't put my foot in it already. Especially when he's been so nice to me.

He shakes his head and makes a face. "No, thanks." He pops a fry into his mouth and chews. "I've got an idea."

I raise my eyebrow and wait.

"Let's play twenty questions. We take turns asking each other anything we want."

"Uh, no," I say firmly. "That sounds like a bad idea."

"Come on," Evan says, bumping me with his shoulder. "If you don't want to answer, just say pass, and we'll come back to that one another time. How else am I supposed to get to know my new neighbor?"

I think about it while I finish the last bite of my burger. Wiping my hands on a napkin, I let out a slow breath. "Okay, but I can pass as much as I want to."

"Sounds fair," he says, smiling like he just won the lottery. "You go first."

"How old are you?" I ask, hoping if I keep the questions light, he will follow suit.

"Twenty-six. My turn." He turns in his seat to fully face me and smiles, popping that dimple out again. "How old are you?"

Good, it's working. "Twenty-six. Same as you. Siblings?"

He nods his head. "One sister named Tracey."

I wait for him to ask me about Keeley.

"Why did you move to Piney Brook, really?" he asks, jumping from the simple sibling question right into the purple of my bruised heart.

"Pass." I turn and look out the passenger side window. "I don't think we should keep playing." I really don't want to get into this with someone I just met. This is a fresh start. A chance to leave the old me and all the baggage behind.

"All right, we'll come back to it another time." Evan doesn't even skip a beat before he slips back into the game coaxing me to do the same. Once he finishes his burger, he puts the trash into the bag and gets the truck back onto the road.

He must sense I'm not ready to open up because after my pass, he sticks to the straightforward stuff. I discover his sister is married with two children. We both like pepperoni pizza and the color green.

"What type of music do you like to listen to?" he asks next.

"Country music is my favorite, especially the newer pop style. Though I won't ever turn off some Garth Brooks or Martina McBride."

He shakes his head and makes a face.

"What about you?"

"Nineties' alternative. I've never been big on country music. It all seems so whiney to me."

"You've just not found the right artist yet," I say, giving him a sly grin.

When we pull into the Furniture Barn parking lot, I realize I know more about my new neighbor than I did about my roommates in college.

"That was interesting." I let myself out and hop down before he gets any ideas about opening my door for me.

Evan frowns and comes to my side.

"I would have gotten your door for you."

"It's all right, I got it." Patrick never bothered opening a door for me. I've always just gotten it myself.

He sighs and motions for me to go first. "Lead the way."

The Furniture Barn is in a building that resembles an old time barn. The wooden siding faded ages ago, and they framed the big front door with faux sliding barn doors. Reaching for the handle, I swing the door open wide and step into the air conditioning.

"Howdy, what can I help ya with?" A burly man with more beard than visible face greets us at the door. His stomach protrudes over his pants, which are being held in place by suspenders that look dangerously close to snapping.

"Hi, I'm Karlee. I'm here to pick up my furniture order." I pull out the receipt from my purse and hand it to him. "I called and spoke to Freddy earlier."

"Ah yes, I remember you." He taps his name tag, grins and scratches his belly. "You'll be better off if you pull around to the side there," Freddy says, pointing to the far side of the building. "That's where the loading is done."

"Thanks."

Evan grabs his keys from his pocket as we step outside. "Hop in, I'll drive us around. Hopefully, they have someone who can help load the furniture so you don't have to." He winks and clicks the button to unlock the truck.

Shaking my head, I climb in and buckle up. "I have no problem helping," I say firmly once he's in the truck. "Besides, how do you think we're getting it up the stairs?"

"I've got a buddy who's coming to help."

My mouth drops open. Not only is he helping me pick up the furniture, he got someone else to help lug it up the stairs.

"Didn't your momma ever tell you not to leave your mouth hanging open? A bug's gonna fly in there." He laughs as I snap my mouth shut.

"I didn't know anyone else was helping. I'd have gotten some money out to pay you guys. As it is, I already owe you." I sigh.

"Nah, you don't owe me, and you don't owe Heath either. We've been friends nearly my whole life. Helping each other out is just what we do."

Evan maneuvers the truck up to the loading space and hops out before I can argue. I watch as he exchanges words with a younger employee than dear ole Freddy. The guy nods and, the next thing I know, he's helping Evan load up my couch and bed onto the truck.

Not going to lie, the idea of having a space to sit and to sleep has me grinning from ear to ear. Watching Evan and his helper load the heavy items into the truck bed is just a bonus. I may have sworn off relationships, but I can appreciate a good-looking man or two, right?

Chapter Four

Evan

Once the furniture's loaded on the back of the truck, I tighten it down with bungee cords. Can't have Karlee's furniture falling out on the side of the highway. I slide my phone out of my pocket and text Heath.

Me: Be there in about an hour. Thanks for the help.

Heath: No problem, man. Happy to help. See ya then.

I slide my phone back into my pocket and hop into the truck. Karlee's grinning bigger than a Cheshire cat, and that's got my heart doing funny things in my chest. She's downright beautiful when she smiles.

"All right, you ready to head home and get your apartment settled finally?" I ask as I start the truck and pull away from the loading zone.

"Yes," she says, excitement making her voice higher than usual. "I can't wait to sleep in my bed. I hope the mattress I picked is comfortable. And my couch, for that matter. I've never picked furniture on my own before."

"Where did you live before you came to Piney Brook?"

"I lived in Rockville, just outside of Little Rock. I've lived with my mom and sister in the same little house my whole life. Well, except for when I was in college." She turns her head away from me and looks out the window.

"Nothing wrong with that," I say, trying to lighten the suddenly heavy mood. "Lots of people live with their parents while they are going to college and getting established. I lived with mine until I'd been working for Brant for almost a year. Took me a while to save up enough."

She turns to face me again and smiles, but this time it looks forced.

"Thanks."

The rest of the drive passes in silence. I've got country music—yuck—playing for her, and she sings along softly. Her attention is focused on something outside the truck. If I had to guess, outside Piney Brook.

Heath is standing at the bottom of the stairs when we drive up. He waves and I roll down the window. "Hey, man, thanks for coming. Help me back it in."

"You got it," Heath says, jogging back to the sidewalk.

He helps direct me into the space since I can't see out my rearview mirror. Once I'm in, I put the truck in park and shut it off. Karlee slides out of her seat and makes her way to the back of the truck.

"Heath, this is my neighbor Karlee. Karlee, my best friend since grade school, Heath."

Heath's gaze roams over Karlee, and I have to bite my tongue not to say something.

"Nice to meet you," he says, taking her hand and bringing it to his lips for a kiss.

"You too," Karlee says. Pink colors her cheeks, and she brushes her hair from her shoulder. "I'll go unlock the door and put Peanut in her carrier. Don't want her running up a tree again."

Heath watches her climb the stairs, a big grin on his face. "Why didn't you tell me your neighbor is gorgeous?"

I punch him in the shoulder. "Dude, leave her alone. She's my neighbor, for crying out loud." I move to unstrap the bungee cords, and he reaches for the other end.

"I didn't think neighbors were off limits, man," he says matter-of-factly. "Remember when you dated my neighbor, Sabrina?" He shakes his head. "That was a nightmare."

"Exactly," I say, pointing my finger at him. "So, stay away."

He laughs and throws his hands in the air. "Message received."

"Wow, you guys, thanks." Karlee turns and flops backwards onto her new bed. "This is going to be the best night ever!"

Heath laughs and extends his hand to help her back up. I roll my eyes. Of course, he's not taking the no flirting with my neighbor rule seriously.

"Happy to help." I grit the words from between clenched teeth. "Heath, we should go. The games already started." I motion toward the front door. "Besides, I'm sure Karlee would like to get her bed made and settle in."

She stands and smiles. "Thanks, really."

I nod and grab Heath's arm, practically dragging him from her room.

"Anytime," he says, waggling his eyebrows. *Who does that?*

She giggles and waves as I push him through her front door and onto the landing.

"Bro," he says, pulling his arm loose. "What's wrong with you?" He raises an eyebrow and stares at me.

"No. Flirting. With. My. Neighbor." I enunciate every word so he hears me clearly. "She's off limits. I get the feeling she left her hometown for some space, not to be hit on."

"Okay, okay." Heath puts his hands up in surrender. "Can't blame me, though. She's gorgeous and sweet, too. Besides, I haven't had a date since I moved home." He shrugs and waits for me to open the door to my apartment.

"Have you called Gabby?" I'm not sure what happened there. Those two were inseparable before he left for the military. Somewhere along the way, something must have happened, because neither one of them will talk about the other.

"Nah," he says, settling into my couch. "She wouldn't want to hear from me, anyway."

"You sure about that?" I ask. He's been home for a few months, but I can tell he's having a tough time adjusting to civilian life. Having another friend to talk to might help.

Heath shrugs and avoids eye contact. Okay . . . "How's your mom?"

"She's good, I think." Heath sighs. "I don't know anymore, man. The treatments are hard on her. It kills me she was going through this alone before I came home."

I pass him a cold Coke, put a bag of chips and a bowl of salsa on the coffee table. "I can't imagine."

"Can we just watch the game? I need a break from the heavy stuff."

"You bet," I say, grabbing a handful of chips and popping one in my mouth.

An hour later, I'm nodding off. The game's pretty much over, and I'm ready for bed. I stand and press my fists into my back, getting a good stretch. "I'm headed to bed, man. Feel free to stay. I can toss you a pillow and a blanket if you want to crash on the couch."

Heath stands and moves to the kitchen to throw his empty can in the recycling bin. "Nah, I'm going to head out. Mom has an early radiation appointment tomorrow."

I slap him gently on the shoulder. "I'm here. Anytime you need a friend."

Heath nods. "Thanks. What I need is to go out this weekend. Get back into the groove of Piney Brook social life." He laughs, but it sounds hollow. "What little of it there is."

The gravel from the parking lot of the Curly Pig crunches under my tires. A neon sign flashes pink to white. The pink shows an outline of a pig, and the white shows the name of Piney Brook's only sports bar—a franchise of the one closer to the University in Fayetteville.

Music floats into the gravel lot every time the swinging front doors open. Weekend nights are busy at the Curly Pig, and not usually my scene.

"Thanks for doing this, man." Heath says, swinging open the passenger door. "I know it's not your thing."

I sigh and adjust my baseball cap. "It's all right. I haven't been here in a while. Getting out is probably good for me."

We approach the swinging doors just as they open. A woman stumbles out, hanging onto the arm of none other than Thatcher Blount, my high school rival. I suck in a breath when I realize the very inebriated woman is, in fact, Louise, my ex.

"Come on, baby," Thatcher says, pulling her closer to his side and eyeing me. "Let's get you home."

Louise giggles and leans into him as she stumbles and almost falls. "Sounds good, lover boy."

My fists ball at my sides. Heath grabs my arm and tugs me through the doors and away from the train wreck that was my life. This is why I don't go out anymore. It's also why I don't date.

"She's still in town?" Heath asks. He leans against the bar and raises his hand to get the bartender's attention. "I was sure they'd left Piney Brook for New York or something."

I sigh and rub my hands over my face. "They came back." I really do not want to talk about Louise and Thatcher. Not now, not ever. Brant and Daniel don't even realize we were once an item. Being several years behind them in school has its perks.

Heath gives me a knowing look and a quick nod. "So," he says, looking around the bar. "Tell me, who's new?"

I scan the bar top and tables that aren't hidden from the small dance floor, which is currently filled with people cutting loose and laughing. In the corner, I spot a group of people from the hospital, and my breath catches. Heath hands me a Coke and follows my line of sight.

"Hey! Karlee's here. We should go say hi!"

Heath's already squeezing between groups of girls who are laughing and dancing wildly to the 90s remix music, when my brain realizes what he just said.

I take the long way around the dance floor, avoiding getting inadvertently turned into an Evan sandwich. As I turn the corner, I see Heath slide into the booth next to Karlee. He makes eye contact with me and grins. I can feel my eyebrows creeping further up my forehead with every step in their direction.

"Here he is," Heath says, raising his cup in my direction. "Evan, look who I found."

He grins and for a moment he reminds me of the twelve-year-old kid who used to sleep over and have video game battles with me. I decide to make the best of this weird night. He deserves one night to be that happy again.

"Hey, guys." I say to the table. "How's it going?"

A chorus of "good" rings out, and I pull up a chair from a nearby table, squeezing it in at the end of the booth.

I lean in and whisper in Karlee's ear, thankful that she made Heath slide between her and some guy I haven't seen around before. "Are you going to introduce me to your friends?" Her cheeks turn a pretty shade of pink, and I fight to swallow the grin that wants to break loose.

"Mona, Terran, Marla, and Nicki."

She points to the people seated across from her at the table. I'm sure they are all great, but all I can see is her. This isn't good. I take a sip of my soda to distract myself from the warm heat that is spreading through my chest. Like warmed honey for a cough, Karlee does something to me.

She shrugs and takes a sip of her fruity looking drink. "This is Evan, my neighbor," she says as she places the drink on the table in front of her.

Mona giggles. "*The* neighbor?" she asks, lifting an eyebrow and smiling.

Karlee's pink cheeks blaze red, and I thank the owners of the Curly Pig for not putting in ridiculously low lighting.

I bump her with my shoulder. "Have you been talking about me?" I chuckle. "All good things, I hope."

The corner of her mouth lifts in a small smile. "So, Marla, weren't you telling us about your run-in with the newest doctor?" she asks, diverting the attention from her. Smooth.

Marla nods. "Dr. Sullivan. He transferred here from somewhere in South Carolina after Christmas last year. From what I hear, he's a very good acute care specialist."

"Thank goodness," Mona pipes in. "It was time for Dr. Ferrick to retire. I swear, he was the ER doctor when my momma was growing up." Everyone laughs.

"I wonder what brought him to Piney Brook," Terran says, looking around the bar. "It's not like we have a lot to offer. He must be in hiding or something to land here." Her eyes land on Karlee, who's focused on picking her napkin apart. "Sorry girl. I grew up here. Never thought I'd stick around."

Heath leans forward and places his elbows on the table. "Take it from me. Leaving isn't as great as it seems." He smiles, but it doesn't quite reach his eyes. He brings his drink to his lips and finishes it. "I think I'm headed to the bar for another round. Anyone want anything?"

Marla asks for a Shirley Temple with extra cherries, and Heath nods. "Anyone else?"

I shake my head no. I don't really drink. Besides, I'm driving. Karlee scoots out of the pleather bench seat and lets him out. I slide in beside her when she scoots back in.

"It'll be easier this way," I say, shrugging. "He will want to move around freely." I wink at her and turn my attention back to Terran. "You grew up here?"

She nods. "I did. I was a freshman when you were a senior." She tips her head back and laughs. "All the girls had a huge crush on you, but they were afraid of Louise."

I must have made a face, because the giggles at the table abruptly stop. "Sorry," Terran says. "I'm really putting my foot in my mouth tonight."

Karlee places her hand on my arm and gives me a gentle squeeze. I appreciate the support. Even if she doesn't know the details. "No problem," I say, forcing a smile. "That was a long time ago."

Chapter Five

Karlee

I KNOW TERRAN DIDN'T mean to press all the wrong buttons, but somehow she found not only my sore spot, but Evan's too. I turn toward the bar and spot Heath chatting with some guys while he's waiting his turn.

"I guess I should have expected to see you here," I say to Evan. "I've been told it's the spot to be on the weekend."

He nods. "Yep, Beats and Eats has a live band sometimes, but everyone funnels over here after they finish around nine." He looks around and shifts in his seat.

"Not a big drinker?"

He looks down at his mostly full glass. "Not really." He frowns. "I don't come here often, but Heath needed a night on the town." He turns his head and nods in Heath's direction. "I'm the designated driver."

"Responsible. A good friend, you are," I say in my best Yoda accent.

Evan laughs, the first genuine laugh I've heard from him tonight. "Wow, quoting the wise green one, you are."

I giggle. "Don't you love those movies? My sister Keeley and I spent a lot of time with our next-door neighbors when we were growing up. They had boys, so we spent a lot of time battling the dark side after school."

"I never saw the appeal," Marla says, capturing my attention.

"No?" I ask. "Why not?"

"Too far-fetched for me. And why did they release the last three movies first? It's confusing." She shrugs and waves her hand in my general direction. "Dark side, light side... people have both, right?"

"I mean... I guess, yeah."

"You didn't like anything about the movies?" Nick asks.

She tilts her head to the side and pauses. After a moment, she giggles. "I guess I liked the little teddy bears and that goofy alien sea dog thing."

I smack my hand to my forehead.

"She did not just say that." Evan groans from beside me.

"Well, I don't remember their names," Marla says and laughs. "You guys are too funny." She points to Mona and Terran. "Back me up. Aren't those movies boring?"

The women shrug and burst out in giggles. "Come on," Mona says. "Let's dance."

I shake my head no, an excuse already on my lips, when Evan takes my hand in his.

"Dance with me?" He looks so sincere, I can't say no. Besides, If I'm dancing with my *friend* Evan, other guys will leave me alone. The way his eyes turned cold at the mention of Louise tells me he isn't looking for a relationship either.

He may give me goosebumps, and be the most handsome and considerate man I've met, but he's firmly in the friend zone. Safe.

"Fine," I say, letting him gently pull me to the dance floor. "But if you step on my toes, I'm showering your apartment in catnip the next time I'm over."

Evan laughs and leans closer to my ear. "You're welcome over anytime, Karlee. You're fun to be around, and you make me laugh."

I suck in a breath and tell my stupid heart to slow down. Friends should be able to make each other laugh. He isn't flirting. He's being friendly.

We dance the next few songs. Never getting too close, but always close enough to ward off any unwanted attention. Evan keeps looking around and keeping tabs on Heath who seems to know everyone in the bar tonight.

"You okay?" I ask when he stutter-steps and misses my toes by an inch.

"I think it's time for me to get Heath out of here." He smiles down at me. "I've had a great time tonight."

I smile back and tuck a piece of loose hair behind my ear. "Me too. Thanks for keeping the vultures away." I tip my head in the direction the girls are dancing. Guys are swarming them, except for Terran who has been dancing with Nick all night. The men in here are like mosquitoes ready to swoop in and bite. "I think I'll head home myself."

"Do you need a ride home?"

"No, I was only drinking cranberry juice tonight." I smile. "Not a drinker either."

Evan laughs and points to the table. "Why don't you tell them you're leaving so they don't worry, then grab your stuff and I'll walk you out."

I nod and turn to get someone's attention. Marla is closest, so I lean in and let her know I'll see her at work this week. She nods and goes right back to dancing.

When I get back to the table, Evan and Heath are in a heated discussion. They both look annoyed, and I debate standing back until they work it out. Heath glances in my direction and his shoulders fall. He waves me over.

"Sorry," he says sullenly. "It's been a while since I let loose."

I shrug and lean into the booth to get my sweater. I locked my purse in my trunk and popped the keys, my ID, and some cash into my pocket. "You don't have to apologize to me."

He grimaces. "I'm going to feel like crap tomorrow."

"How much did you drink?" Evan asks.

I'd say he's overreacting, but maybe he knows something I don't. Heath definitely seems like he is a bit more than tipsy, but he isn't fall-down drunk like that girl I saw being helped out by her boyfriend when Evan and Heath got here.

"I'm fine," Heath says. "I'm not her, Evan. I'm of age, and you are driving."

Evan blows out a long breath. "You're right," he says. "Sorry."

"I get it, man. You need to let that go. Not everyone is going to get drunk and run off the road. Give me some credit." Heath pats Evan's arm and then walks toward the exit.

"Everything okay?" I ask hesitantly.

"It will be." Evan sighs. "Come on, I'll walk you out." He gives Heath a pointed look, and motions for him to follow us out.

Evan keeps his hand at the small of my back as he walks me toward the door. It feels nice. I don't remember a time Patrick ever made me feel protected when we were out.

The warm night air wraps me in an envelope of damp heat when we walk outside. "I can't believe how humid it is tonight."

Evan tips his nose up and sniffs. "Rain is coming. That should help cool it down some."

I giggle. "Did you really just sniff the air to see if it was going to rain?"

He nods, a serious look on his face. "How else would you know if it was going to rain?"

I pull my phone out of my back pocket and wave it around. "It's called a weather app."

He shakes his head. "Unreliable."

I shake my head and chuckle. "As opposed to your sniff method?"

He pins me with a stare. "I'll have you know I have a very sensitive nose. It can tell me things." He taps his face just to the side of his left nostril.

"Uh, okay. You have a psychic nose." I raise an eyebrow and take a step back. "Maybe I should have taken my chances with the vampire mosquitos inside."

He laughs. "No, seriously. Pay attention. You'll learn when it smells like rain, too."

I feel my eyes go wide and my forehead crease as I nod my head. "Okay, whatever you say." I wink to let him know I'm not really freaked out. It is strange though. Who claims they can smell the rain?

I open the door to my SUV and slide inside. "Thanks for walking me out. I'll see you."

He smiles and nods, before walking to his truck where Heath's leaned against the side. Heath laughs and Evan glances back in my direction just as I'm putting the car in reverse. He gives a little wave, and I wave back before pulling out of the space and heading home.

Sunday afternoon, I make myself some tea, and settle in to call my family. Dialing my sister first, I wait while it rings through.

"Karlee!" Keeley yells. "I've been waiting for you to call today!"

"Hi, Keels," I say, laughing at her excitement. "You seem awfully excited."

She giggles, and I smile. She's always been the more bubbly sister.

"I have some news," she says. "I'm engaged!" She squeals, and I have to pull the phone from my ear.

For a moment, a pang of jealousy hits low in my gut, but I shake it off. "I'm so happy for you, Keels! Tell me all about it."

I listen as Keeley details the way Scott proposed. Her excitement is contagious.

"That's so wonderful," I say as she wraps up the proposal story. "Have you guys talked about setting a date? Are you thinking next summer?"

She hesitates.

"Keels, have you picked a date?" I repeat.

"Yeah, this August."

"Wow," I say, surprised they are doing it so soon. "That's less than two months away."

"I know, but we already know we want to keep it low key. We want to be married and get an apartment off campus together this year before Scott starts his Master's program."

"I'm sure it will all come together. I'm so happy for you," I say again.

"Thanks, Karlee. I know it's short notice, but I really want you to be there," Keeley pleads.

"I don't think I can swing being there long enough to be a part of the wedding party, but I wouldn't miss it for the world," I reassure her.

"Thanks. I couldn't get married without you there."

I smile and hold the phone closer to my ear. We speak for a few more minutes, then I promise to call her again soon.

I take a deep breath and prepare for the onslaught of wedding-planning excitement I'm sure will greet me when I call Mom.

Before I even hear it ring, she answers. "Did you hear?"

"I did," I say, laughing. "Hi, Mom."

"Oh, Karlee, I have so much to do!" She takes a breath and laughs. "It's a good thing Scott and Keeley want something simple. Have you considered who you'll be bringing to the wedding?"

"Bringing?" I ask. I hadn't even considered a plus-one.

"Why don't you invite the nice guy you're always talking about?" Mom says slyly.

"Mom, he's just a friend." I roll my eyes. Not that she can see.

"Well, it's a thought," she says. "Besides, having a friend with you might be nice. Especially since you know how our family can be."

Ugh, she's right. I can see it now, everyone feeling sorry for me on what's supposed to be Keeley's special day. "I'll think about it."

Finally, I get off the phone, after promising to consider asking Evan to be my plus-one. The calls took up more of my day than I'd planned. I barely have time to shower before heading to work.

"Hey, girl," Marla says when I walk behind the nurse's station. "Looks like you managed to catch yourself a fine fish the other night." She winks at me and fans her face.

"He's my neighbor, and he walked me to my car. That's it," I say, feeling the heat bloom on my chest. For once, I'm thankful this hospital prefers scrubs without a V-neck.

"What is it?" Mona asks, sliding behind the counter of the nurses' station. "Don't keep me in the dark!"

"She claims there's nothing between her and the hottie neighbor she was dancing with Friday night." Marla points at me. "Chemistry. So much chemistry. If you don't want to explore that, I will."

Mona cackles. "I'll give it a go. He was always the hottest guy in school, and he only had eyes for Louise. Though, now that I think about it, I'm not sure he ever looked at her the way he was looking at you." She puts her finger to her cheek and tilts her head. "Hey, Terran," she calls.

"Yeah," Terran says, stepping out of the linen closet holding a pillow and blanket.

"Do you remember Evan in high school?"

"Duh," she says, laughing. "Hottest guy in the senior class."

Marla looks at me with an *I told you so* grin. "And would you say he only had eyes for Louise?"

Terran leans her hip on the outside of the nurse's station wall. "Oh, yeah. He was smitten. Even though that girl didn't deserve it." She shakes her head. "What a mess."

Marla nods her head in agreement. "I know, but did you catch how he was checking out our newest nurse?"

Mona's eyes about pop out of her face. "Oh my gosh, now that you mention it..." She looks at me and narrows her eyes. "Are you two together?"

I laugh and put my hands up in a defensive gesture. "Nope. Just friendly neighbors." I back away slowly and put my purse on the shelf below the countertop. "Now, is someone going to give me a report?"

Thankfully, the rest of my shift goes smoothly. No one mentions Louise, Evan, or his eyes again. Just before the close of shift, we got a new patient sent up from the ER. As I was doing the admittance paperwork and getting the patient settled in their room, I noticed the admitting physician from the ER was Dr. Sullivan. I still hadn't met the elusive doctor that had everyone whispering. Apparently, he was the best thing since sliced bread and handsome enough to be an underwear model. How anyone would know that from scrubs and a physician's coat, I have no idea.

The patient was being admitted for a kidney stone. Poor guy. Kidney stones are brutal. Thankfully, the medicine they gave him in the ER seems to be working. "Get some rest, Mr. Trenton. I'll come check on you in a while. Just press the call button if you need anything."

Mr. Trenton has been dozing on and off since he got into his room. "Thanks," he whispered, nodding off. I flip the light switch off and gently pulled his door closed behind me. I like that Piney Brook General only doubles patients if they have to. Most of the time, being a small-town hospital, people get their own room. If I were a patient, I'd appreciate the privacy.

By 6:55 a.m. I'm watching the clock. As soon as I give my report, I'm out of here. My charting is done, and I am exhausted.

Terran walks into the nurse's station and hands me a large hot coffee. "From the Coffee Loft next door." She sets her coffee on the counter and tucks her purse away. "How was your shift?"

I yawn and pull my arms above my head in a stretch. "Good. Mostly uneventful. We had one new admittance. Mr. Trenton in room four. Kidney stones. He was asleep when I checked on him about thirty minutes ago. It will be time for his meds soon, and I'm sure he will be asking."

She shudders. "Kidney stones are the worst."

I finish giving her the rundown between sips of the coffee she brought me. "Thanks for this," I say, holding up the cup. "It's delicious."

"You're welcome. I didn't know what you liked, so I just got it with cream and sugar. You should pop in there. They have donuts and gourmet coffee flavors. It's a franchise, but they offer local favorites on the menu." She grins. "I probably spend too much money there, but it's good."

I laugh. "I get it. A good cup of coffee is hard to find in a hospital." I gather my purse and water bottle. "Hey, do you happen to know a good hairdresser? I haven't had my hair done in a long time. I'm way overdue." Especially with Keeley's wedding coming up.

Terran looks up from the computer where she is checking med schedules. "Oh, that's easy. Anne Masters down at Cozy Cuts & More. She's literally the best. Her aunt owns the salon, but she's pretty much retired, so Anne runs it now."

"Great, thanks," I say, adjusting my messy bun. "I'll give her a call."

As I walk to my car, I can't stop smiling. It's about time I did something for myself.

Chapter Six

Evan

Mittens darts behind the couch when he spies the cat carrier resting on the kitchen table. "Come on, Mittens," I call, hoping the soft tone of my voice will trick him into cooperating. "Here kitty, kitty. Don't you want to go to Aunt Tracey's?"

His nose pokes from behind the couch. I reach out to him slowly, and the ringtone of my cell phone pierces the air causing Mittens to shriek and disappear further into the crack behind the couch.

"Dang it!" I reach in my pocket and grab my phone, swiping to answer without bothering to see who it is. "What?" I snap, standing up from the crouched position beside the couch.

"Evan?" my sister asks hesitantly.

I drop my head into my free hand and sigh. "Sorry. Mittens is hiding and if I don't get a move on, I won't have time to drop him off at your house before I leave."

"About that," Tracey says over the intensifying crying in the background. "Brody just fell off the couch, and I've got to take him to the ER. I think he broke his arm. Mom's on her way to watch Emelia, but I just don't think I can take on Mittens right now, too.

This kid is trying to give me a heart attack, or cause us to file bankruptcy—whichever comes first. We've been to the ER three times this year."

I fall back onto the sofa and sigh. "No problem, Trace. I hope Brody's okay."

"Thanks, Evan." She sighs. "I'd say ask Mom, but you know how she is about animals."

"I know," I say, already thinking of a back-up plan. Maybe Heath will watch him. "I'll think of something. Don't worry about me. Take care of Brody. Let me know what they say."

After she promises to keep me posted, I hang up the phone and text Daniel to go ahead without me. We were supposed to carpool, but I'll have to find someone for Mittens before I can leave for the lake.

Lying back on the couch, I close my eyes and think. The soft feeling of Mittens climbing on top of me and curling into my chest serves to both soothe and irritate me.

"Hey, buddy." I run my hand over his soft fur and his kitty purr engine starts rumbling. "Now you come out?"

A soft knock on the door startles him, and the moment is over. Shaking my head, I stand and wipe the cat hair off of my shirt before opening the door.

"Karlee, hey," I say, surprised to see her so early in the day. Her night shifts at the hospital usually mean she sleeps most of the day.

"Hey, are you busy?" She wipes her hands down her jeans and shifts from side to side like she's nervous.

"Is everything okay?" I ask, opening the door wider for her to come through.

She comes inside and looks around. "Yes, I just had a question." She glances at me, and I see her mentally calculating.

I take her elbow and gently guide her to the couch. After she sits, I head to the kitchen and grab her a glass of water. Taking a seat next to her, I hand it to her. "What's up, sunshine?"

She gulps from the glass as though she's been stranded in the desert, and not across the hall in her air-conditioned apartment.

"Well, I recently found out my sister is getting married," she says, looking down at her hands.

"Okay," I say. "Isn't that a good thing?"

She grins. "The best thing, really. Scott is so good to her, and I know she's been hoping he'd ask."

I lean back into the cushions and wait.

"The thing is..." She pauses and takes a deep breath. "Well, what I wanted to ask is..."

"Karlee, it's me. You can ask me anything," I say, hoping it reassures her.

"Well, I was wondering if you'd be my plus-one. To my sister's wedding," she blurts. "I mean, you probably can't get off work, and it's soon, and we're just friends..."

She's rambling, and it's the cutest thing I've ever seen.

"Karlee," I say, trying to break through her steady stream of excuses. "Karlee," I say again, reaching over and grabbing her hand.

She finally stops talking and looks at me, her face a shade of pink I've never seen before. "I'd love to."

Her mouth drops open before she snaps it shut. "I didn't even tell you when it is," she says. "Plus, it's in Rockville."

I nod. "I figured," I say, shrugging. "I'm sure I can get the time off. It's fine." I stand up and move to the calendar hanging on the side of the fridge. "When is it?" I ask, grabbing a pen from the cup I keep on the counter.

"It's the first Saturday in August." She stands and brings her cup to the sink. "Seriously Evan, if you can't make it, it's no big deal," she says, pouring the ice down the drain. "I just thought I'd ask."

I mark the weekend she said on the calendar and grin. "I'll talk to Brant this week, but I'm sure I can get the time off."

"Well, I'll go. I don't want to take up more of your time." She moves toward the door and stops. "Where are you going?" she asks, pointing to the suitcase by the door.

"Nowhere, unless I can find someone to watch Mittens," I say, before explaining the situation.

"I can watch him," she says. "It's the least I could do. You've done so much for me since I moved here." She bends down to pet Mittens, who has finally decided to stop hiding.

"Okay," I say quickly. "Are you sure?"

She nods. "It's no problem."

"I've got a spare key here," I say, pulling the key out of the junk drawer and handing it to her. "And the food and things are on the table. Mittens is easy. He only requires the standard cat care." I grab my phone and open the contacts. "Here, put your number in, and I'll call your phone. That way, you have my number in case anything comes up."

I pass her the phone and wait for her to punch her number in. She hands it back, and I hit call letting it ring through to voicemail.

"Don't you need to get going?" she asks, picking Mittens up and burying her face in his fur. "We'll be fine."

"Thanks," I say, leaning in and kissing her on the cheek. "I appreciate this. Oh, and Karlee? I love the hair." Grabbing my suitcase, I step out onto the landing and touch my fingers to my tingling lips. Being her plus-one might be a challenge. Like my favorite candy, she's becoming hard to resist.

I get to the lake house around the same time Daniel and Elli do, so I don't feel so bad about getting a late start.

"Hey, sorry I didn't ride down with you. My sister called. Brody hurt himself, so she couldn't take Mittens." I help Daniel unload the back of his truck while his daughter, Elli, bounces around excitedly.

"No worries, did you find someone to watch him?" he asks, passing Elli a sparkly rainbow-colored suitcase with a unicorn on the front.

"Yeah, Karlee's watching him for me." I can't help the smile that lifts my lips.

"Karlee, huh?" Daniel asks, raising an eyebrow at me. "Seems like you guys are getting along well."

"I'd hope so," I say, and laugh. "We're neighbors after all." My lips tingle at the memory of them pressed against her cheek.

He slaps me on the shoulder. "Whatever you say, man."

We make our way inside and find the rest of the gang is already here.

"Better get unloaded," Brant says to me and Daniel. Leaning in, he plants a soft kiss on Morgan's cheek. "Why don't the two of you check on the kids and make sure we actually have beds to sleep in tonight?" he asks, pointing toward Reese.

We head out to help Brant unload his truck and bring everything inside.

"Hey, while I have you," I say, popping the latch on the tailgate and lowering the bed. "Can I have a few days off in August?"

Brant looks at me, studying my face. "Everything okay? You never ask for time off."

I rub my neck, suddenly feeling uncomfortable. I don't know that I'm ready to admit to being Karlee's plus-one to her sister's wedding, but I've got to tell him something. He's right. I don't ask for time. Brant is generous with his days off, and my family is all close. No need to take a bunch of time off. I'd rather work and save the money for a down payment on a house one day.

"Yeah," I sigh. "Karlee had something come up in her hometown, and I offered to help her."

Brant grins. "You sure there's nothing there?"

Daniel chuckles. "Seems like she's caught your attention, Ev."

I shake my head. "Nah, just friends. She just came out of a bad relationship and you know I don't date." Though I'm starting to think if I did, she'd be the kind of girl I'm looking for.

I grab the cooler and pull it to the edge of the tailgate. "Let's get unloaded so we can get to the fun part."

After getting everything unloaded into the correct rooms, the guys and I offer to take the kids on a walk and inspect the lake access and the water amenities in the shed. After a while, we hang out by the water's edge while Daniel shows Elli and Liam, Brant and Morgan's son, how to skip rocks.

"It's funny," I say to the guys. "The things I enjoyed about the lake as a kid are some of the same things I enjoy now."

"Just wait until you have kids of your own," Daniel says. "There's something about seeing the excitement through a child's eyes that brings the fun to a deeper level."

"Speaking of," Brant says, rocking back on his heels. "I, uh, well... that is... Morgan and I..." He rubs his hand on the back of his neck and drops his arms to his sides heavily. "Well, we're thinking about having another kid."

"Whoa! That's huge." I'd wondered if they would want to expand their family.

“Babies are wonderful, Brant. Even if they are exhausting at first,” Daniel says and laughs.

Brant grins. “It’s just something we are thinking about right now, but I’m excited.”

“Hey, guys,” Morgan calls from the porch. “Why don’t you come inside and get changed? I was thinking the kids might like to swim a bit before dinner.”

“YEAH!” Liam and Elli yell, dropping the rocks they’re holding into a pile and racing toward the house.

Guess we’re going swimming.

Chapter Seven

Karlee

"Well, Mittens. Looks like it's me, you, and Peanut for the next week. I hope you two get along." Mittens purrs and rubs his face against my chin.

I decide to try Mittens in my apartment before taking all of his things over. No need to stress him out. "Let's go explore and meet a new friend, shall we?"

I pick up the key lying on the counter. With Mittens securely in my arms, I open the door and step into the landing. "It's okay, sweet boy," I croon. I close and lock Evan's door and head across the hall to my apartment.

Once inside, I sit on the floor with Mittens in my arms. "Peanut, here, kitty, kitty." Peanut cautiously steps closer, sniffing the air. "It's Mittens. A new friend for you this week." The cats size each other up and then Peanut runs off to her cat tree. She climbs to the top and hides inside the little cubby. Her face pokes out the hole, watching.

"Looks like she's not in the mood to play, Mittens." He yowls and stretches in my arms, so I let him go. I watch from my spot on the floor as he inspects my apartment before finally hopping onto the back of the couch and settling in.

"Thank goodness you two get along," I say when it seems like they've made a truce. Standing, I brush the hair off of my clothes. "That will make this week a lot easier."

I step out to get Mittens's things from across the hall. May as well get everyone settled now. Coming back in the door, I notice Mittens is now on the cat tree with Peanut. Good. I put his water and food bowls down on the other side of the kitchen, giving them some space.

I have the day off, so I decide to do laundry and clean up, keeping the cats company while they feel each other out. I've just put the last load of clothes in the dryer when I hear my phone ringing in the living room.

Grabbing for my phone, I check the caller ID. Evan.

"Hello?" I ask, hoping I don't sound as out of breath as I feel.

"Hello, sunshine." His rich voice coming through the speaker makes me shiver. "How is everyone settling in?"

"Mittens and Peanut?" I ask, wondering why he's calling to check in already.

"Are they getting along?"

"Oh, yeah," I say.

"Great. Mittens is usually good with other animals, but I wanted to make sure." Evan's rich deep voice causes goosebumps to erupt on my arms.

He's only calling to check on his cat. Get a grip, Karlee. "They're doing great so far," I say.

"I talked to Brant. He said I can have as much time off as I need."

"He did? You've already asked him?" I ask. I still feel a bit embarrassed about causing him the trouble.

"Of course. It's already the last week of June. August will be here before we know it, sunshine." He laughs. "To be honest, I'm kind of looking forward to it."

My heart blooms with warmth. "Thank you," I say. "For offering to be my date. Well, my plus-one," I amend. "It will certainly make my life a lot easier to have a friend with me for this fiasco."

Evan chuckles. "I wouldn't have offered if I wasn't sure. I'm glad you consider me a friend, sunshine."

"Why do you keep calling me that? And of course I do. You've been so nice to me since I moved here." The other nurses at work have taken me into their fold, but they talk too much for me to feel comfortable sharing much with them yet.

"I'm glad. It's good to have friends." Evan mumbles something to someone else. "Sorry, I've got to run. These kids are itching to have fun."

"No problem. Thanks for calling."

"You can put Mittens in my apartment when you work if you don't want to leave them alone together. Talk to you later," he says before the line goes dead.

I sit back on the couch and stare at the phone. I'm taking Evan to my sister's wedding.

Wednesday afternoon, I'm watching reality TV when my phone rings. I snatch it off the coffee table and grin when I see who's calling.

"Hello," I say quickly.

"Hey, sunshine. How's it going?" Evan's voice instantly awakens the sleeping butterflies in my stomach, and I fight to tamp down the feeling. He's a friend, nothing more.

"It's going well," I say. "Mittens and Peanut spent some time chasing a laser light today. I wonder why cats think that's so fun?"

Evan laughs. "Who knows? Probably helps them train to take over the world one day."

I chuckle. "I suppose you're right. How's the lake?"

Evan shares the events of the day. I laugh as he recounts the kids' antics at the lake. He asks me about work, and my sister's wedding plans, and before I realize it, it's late.

"I should go," I say reluctantly, gently touching my fingers to my cheeks which are aching from smiling so much.

"All right, sunshine. I'll call you again soon."

The rest of the week passes quickly. Evan calls almost every day to check on Mittens. It's sweet. We also spend time talking about everything and nothing, including Patrick and Celine's betrayal. It's nice to have a friend who is genuinely interested in how my day went.

Patrick and Celine never wanted to know about the things I dealt with at work. They said it was depressing. Some cases were, sure, but most of the time, it turned out for the better. Everyone needs someone to decompress with. Sometimes it scares me how easy Evan is to talk to, and how quickly he has fallen into that role. Best friend. Is that possible?

Mittens is in my lap kneading my legs like fresh dough. Peanut has climbed up on the back of the couch and is sleeping behind my head. These two have gotten along like peanut butter and jelly this week.

I snort. Peanut butter and jelly. Poor Peanut, she'd been so small when I adopted her from the shelter that she looked like a little peanut still in its shell. I'd meant to find her a better name, but *Peanut* stuck.

"Evan comes home today," I tell Mittens as I caress his fur. "I bet you'll be happy to be home with him." Mittens turns a circle and curls into a ball.

I look at my phone, sitting on the arm of the couch. I pull up my mom's number and hit call.

"Karlee," Mom says as soon as she answers the phone.

"Hey, Mom," I say.

"Have you decided on a plus-one yet?" she asks, getting right to the point. "I'm trying to finalize the guest list, and we need a head count for the caterer."

I sigh. "I've asked a friend, but I'm not sure yet, Mom. Something may come up. Can't you just put me down for two and if I don't bring anyone, I'll take a doggy bag." I laugh, trying to diffuse the situation.

"Karlee, you know you don't get a doggy bag at a wedding." She huffs.

"It was a joke," I say, still laughing.

She sighs. "Sorry, there are so many details, and the days are flying by."

"It's okay, Mom. I know you have a full plate right now."

"What have you been up to this week?" she asks.

I'm grateful for the change in topic. Though I'm happy for my sister, I still feel a little jealous that it's not me getting married and settling down right now. "I'm cat-sitting for the neighbor," I say, glancing over to the cat tree where Mittens and Peanut have spent most of their time this week.

A knock at my door startles Mittens, who jumps off the cat tree and runs behind the couch.

"Hey, Mom. I hate to cut you short, but someone is knocking on my door. I've got to run." After our goodbyes, I stand and move to the door. Pressing up to my tiptoes I peek through the peephole. The first thing I see is Evan's gorgeous grin, and the dimple popping out in his cheek.

I take a deep breath and swing open the door. "Hey, you're back!"

Evan's grin grows wider, pushing that adorable dimple further into place. "I am," he says, still smiling. "Were you not expecting me?"

It's then I remember I'm still in my pajamas. Pink pants and a matching shirt with coffee cups and kittens all over them. I laugh. "I guess I forgot to get dressed today."

"It's cute."

I step back and open the door further. "Come on in." I wave my hand toward the living room.

He steps inside and slides off his shoes. "Thanks. How was he?"

"Great," I say, pointing to the cat tree in the corner where Peanut is nestled into a soft bed. "They spent most of their week on the cat tree, but Mittens just ran behind the couch when you knocked."

"Oh my, a kitty castle. He'll never want to come home now." Evan slips off his shoes and heads over to the couch, getting down on his hands and knees, he peers into the space behind the couch. "Here kitty, kitty," he coos. Mittens hesitantly sticks his head out from behind the couch, and Evan scoops Mittens from his hiding place, then cuddles him close.

Swoon.

"How was your trip?"

"Great," Evan says, walking over to the cat tree to pet Peanut, too. "It was really relaxing to spend some time outdoors. It was also nice to get to know a new friend better." He looks at me and winks.

"I'm glad," I say, trying not to melt on the spot. Has he always been this handsome, or has the wedding date thing already started messing with my head? I'm going to have to be careful. Those hours on the phone this week have already made me way too happy.

"Thanks for watching him. I really appreciate it," he says, nuzzling Mittens again. "Poor Tracey. Brody's having a hard time with the cast on his arm. He's already given Emelia a few bruises." He shakes his head. "That kid doesn't realize how rough he is."

"Little kids usually don't," I remind him.

"True. Listen, my friends are having a Fourth of July cookout. Do you want to come? No pressure."

"Thanks for the invite, but I can't. I am scheduled to work." I find I'm disappointed I can't go, though.

"No worries, just figured I'd ask. I'll take Mittens and get out of your hair. You work tonight, right?" Evan asks.

"Yep," I say, pointing to my jammies. "I should start getting ready."

Evan nods. "Unless the hospital has a new dress code, you might want to." He grins and slides his shoes back on at the front door. "See ya, sunshine."

"Bye," I say, closing the door after he leaves. My apartment smells like his cologne—spicy, sweet, and outdoorsy. It reminds me of when I slept in his bed—which makes the heat rise in my cheeks and I sigh. Why does he have to smell so good?

Chapter Eight

Evan

Back in my apartment, I can't help but grin. Somehow, Karlee has gotten under my skin. I'd only meant to call and check on Mittens once since she'd never watched him before, but her sweet voice on the phone had me calling nearly every day.

Sometime during the week, talking to her became the highlight of my day. She is incredibly easy to talk to, and her sense of humor matches mine. Hearing her laugh at the end of the day made me wish she was there beside me. She makes me want to try dating again.

Louise was a mess, and I was too young to realize it. Being around Brant and Morgan this week, and seeing Daniel put himself out there and finally get the girl, made me realize I don't want to be alone forever.

Mom was right. I'd closed myself off to the possibility of moving on. Karlee captured my attention the day she moved in. Being her date at her sister's wedding will be weird, but it may be my chance to show myself, and her, what it would be like if we gave it a shot. A trial run of sorts. No harm, no foul if it doesn't work out.

"We aren't like that Patrick dude, are we Mittens? And she's not Louise."

I put him on the floor, and he immediately runs for the bedroom. "Really? Right for my pillow, huh?" Laughing, I open the bag that Karlee put the bowls and extra food into, and get him resettled.

Once Mittens is all set, I move on to unpacking the suitcase I dropped off in my apartment before picking him up from Karlee's. I look at the pile of dirty clothes I've just unloaded into the hamper. Why do vacations create so much laundry?

Throwing a load into the washer, I head to the kitchen to find something for dinner. Unfortunately, there aren't many options. I sigh and close the fridge. Pizza it is.

My phone rings from the other room. Afraid it's Tracey calling to tell me Brody has hurt himself again, I jog to grab it.

"What's up, man?" I ask, slightly out of breath.

"Uh, are you busy?" Daniel asks. "I have pizza."

"Come on over," I say. "See you soon." That solves the dinner problem.

A few minutes later, there's a knock at my door. "Hey," I say, pulling the door open with Mittens snuggled into my chest. Man, I missed him. "What's up? Didn't you just spend days with me? I mean, I know I'm great and all, but..." I close the door behind Daniel as he steps through and places the pizza on the table.

"Yeah, yeah," he shrugs. "I had plans with Elli and Reese, but it didn't work out."

"How do you mean?" I ask, stepping into the kitchen and grabbing some paper plates. I pass Daniel one and flip open the lid of the pizza box. "There's Coke and water in the fridge. Help yourself."

Daniel heads to the fridge and grabs a Coke.

"What do you mean, they didn't work out?" I ask again, sitting down with my food.

"Well, when I got home, Heather was waiting. She came back a week early and missed Elli."

"That's understandable." I nod, taking a huge bite of pizza as I settle back into the couch. "Okay, and Reese?"

Daniel grabs two slices of pizza and the can of Coke. "I was met at the door by her mother."

I look at him for a second, swallow my food, and then burst out laughing. "Oh man, how'd that go?"

"Well, I'm here eating cold pizza with you, so..."

"Dang, that stinks. I thought that kind of stuff only happened in high school." I take another bite of my pizza. "I was just going to watch the game tonight and order pizza, anyway. You're welcome to hang out here."

"Thanks," Daniel says, settling back into the couch.

We watch the game in a comfortable silence until finally Daniel decides to head home. I feel bad for him. I'd be disappointed if my plans were so epically derailed, too. I wonder what it will be like to meet Karlee's family. Even if we aren't together, it's important to me to make a good impression. We are friends, after all. And if they're anything like Karlee, I know I'll love them.

I lock the front door after Daniel leaves and flip off the lights. I step into the little laundry room off the bathroom and throw the clothes from the washer into the dryer before heading to the bathroom to get ready for bed. I haven't washed my sheets since Karlee slept here. Gross, I'm sure, but the smell of vanilla and Karlee is comforting. I make a mental note to wash my sheets this week and find another way to get my Karlee fix.

I pull into the driveway late. I hate being late to family dinner, but I couldn't help it. Heath needed someone to talk to, and I wasn't about to turn him down. He's been through a lot in the last year. Probably longer, considering he'd been deployed for a while before his mom was diagnosed.

"Are you sure your parents won't mind me coming with you? This is a family thing." Heath looks unsure of himself.

"Are you kidding? Mom's been asking when she gets to see you again. You know you became family years ago, man." He spent almost every weekend at our house while his mom worked.

"Yeah, I guess," he says.

I pull into the driveway and park beside Tracey's minivan. I wonder if Lawrence is in town. Family dinners are always better when we are all together.

"Seriously, it's not a problem," I say, turning off the truck and unfastening my seatbelt. Mom's on the porch before I can even get the door open. "The welcoming committee is out." I laugh.

Heath and I get out and make our way up the walk. I lean in and give Mom a peck on her cheek. "Hey, Ma."

"Hey, yourself," she says playfully, swatting me with her dishtowel. "Why didn't you tell me my other son was coming for dinner?"

"It's my fault, Mrs. Thompson. I'm sorry." Heath drops his head—the weight of the world has been on his shoulders lately.

"None of that, Heath. You know you're always welcome." She pulls him into a bear hug and kisses his cheek. "It's been too long since I fed you." She steps back and looks at him a moment. "How's your mom?"

"She's tired today but doing okay. We'll know more soon. The doctors are hopeful." Heath sighs and shoves his hands in his pockets.

Mom pats his shoulder and motions for the front door. "Well, come on in. Dinner's just about done."

We step inside, just in time to see Lawrence grab Brody around the waist and lift him into the air. Giggles fill the air, and I grin. "Good to see you!" I say, making my way to where he still has Brody in the air. "It's been a while."

Lawrence brings Brody back down and sets him on the ground. Emelia is tugging on his leg, so he lifts her into his arms and blows a raspberry on her belly. "I know. Work's been wild, but I shouldn't have to travel again for a while."

He shifts Emelia to his left hip and reaches out his hand to Heath. "Nice to see you again, Heath."

Heath takes his hand and shakes. "Thanks. You too."

"Well, look at this," my dad's voice booms from the entryway. "All my boys in one place. How'd I get so lucky?"

"Hey, Mr. Thompson," Heath says before sticking his hand out to shake.

Dad looks from his outstretched hand to me. I shrug.

"None of that, son. You know you can call me *Dad*." Dad pulls Heath in for a hug, slapping him on the back. "Good to see you."

Heath's voice breaks when he responds. "Thanks."

"Come on now," Tracey calls from the kitchen. "Dinner's going to get cold."

Mom's already put another spot at the table for Heath next to me, and we all sit down. "Go ahead. Fill your plates," she says after Dad says the blessing.

It's quiet while everyone gets settled and starts eating. "Tracey, you said you had some news," Mom says, taking a sip of her sweet tea. "Care to share now?"

Dad grins from his spot at the head of the table. "News, huh?"

Lawrence clears his throat and looks at Tracey. They do that silent communication thing married couples do before he turns and looks at Mom.

"Well, as you know, I've been traveling for work. A lot."

Murmurs of agreement follow his statement.

"I've decided I don't want to be away anymore. Especially now that Tracey is pregnant again." He grins as the table erupts in cheers.

"A baby!" Mom squeals as though this isn't her third grandbaby. "Oh, Tracey! Why didn't you say anything?"

Dad is up and slapping Lawrence on the back. "Well done, son." He laughs. "So, tell us about the travel."

"Well, like I was saying. I don't want to be gone that long anymore. It's too hard on Tracey, and I miss her and the kids too much. I've decided to take another position with the company. Same pay and benefits, but not as much travel. We decided me being home was more important right now than climbing the corporate ladder."

"Oh, my." Mom is wiping tears from her eyes. "I think that is just wonderful."

"I'm happy for you, sis," I manage to get in finally.

"Thanks."

"That's great," Heath says, but his smile doesn't quite reach his eyes. "Babies are wonderful."

I look at him, and for the first time, I wonder if there's more to his stress than his mom's illness.

The rest of the night passes with everyone taking guesses on the baby's gender and discussing name possibilities. For a moment, I imagine Karlee pregnant, and I grin. She'd be such a beautiful pregnant woman.

I shake my head to clear those thoughts. That's not a road I'm ready to go down right now. Or ever.

Heath is quiet, not really joining in the conversation. Mom keeps glancing his way, a look of concern causing her brows to crease.

When he called me earlier, he'd just run into Gabby at Beats and Eats. From what I gathered, she wasn't thrilled to see him. I wish I knew what had happened between those two, but Heath is tight-lipped about it.

After dessert, Tracey and Lawrence decide to pack it up and head home. The kids are getting tired.

"We'd better get going too," I say, standing up and stretching my back. "It's a short week, with the holiday, but we've got a lot of last-minute work scheduled at the shop."

Mom comes out from the kitchen and hands Heath a wrapped plate. "For your mom," she says, patting his hand.

Heath nods, leaning in to drop a kiss on her cheek. "Thanks."

After saying our goodbyes, we hop in the truck and head to Heath's house. A brick townhouse located just on the north side of town with a welcoming red door. The landscaping is a bit lackluster since his mom's been sick. The rose bushes are overgrown, and the annuals she always planted are missing. I wonder if Heath needs help getting it back in shape. I'm sure his mom would enjoy that.

"Thanks for tonight," Heath says when I pull to a stop in his driveway. "Mom will love the leftovers." He holds up the plate Mom made him. "I'll be sure to get this back to you."

"No worries, man." I hesitate, unsure how much to pry. "If there's ever anything you want to discuss, about your time over there, or your mom, or anything, really, you know I'm here, right?"

Heath nods. "Yeah, okay."

"I mean it. I get the feeling you're holding back, and I want you to know I've got your back. Even if all I can do is listen."

Heath looks at me. His mouth opens and closes. "Thanks." He finally says. "I better get this inside." He turns on his heel and heads for his house.

I wait a minute after the door closes before pulling away and heading home.

Chapter Nine

Karlee

I WOKE UP THIS morning to a message from my mother that immediately ruined the good mood I was in.

Apparently, Patrick feels badly about how things ended and wants to apologize in person. So she gave him my address. My address. Who does that?

I'm fuming. I've been up for hours, and can't manage to calm down enough to call and ask her what she was thinking.

As if my thoughts summoned her, my phone rings—her picture pops up on the screen. I swipe to answer. "Mother, what on earth were you thinking?" I start.

"Well, hello, dear," she responds. "I'm guessing you got my message? I thought it would be nice if you two cleared the air once and for all so you can have closure."

I groan. "Mother. The whole point of moving away was to get space. Why on earth would he even want to come all the way to Piney Brook now?"

Mom huffs. "He said he wanted to apologize in person. I thought that was very respectable. Besides, you never know. This could be a chance to rekindle your romance. You know, a real-life second chance."

"Mom, that's only for romance novels. Not for lying, cheating pigs."

Mom scoffs. "That's not true," she insists. "How was I supposed to know you'd be upset? You spent so much time hoping to take your relationship to the next level. He seems genuine," she says as if that is supposed to make this any better.

My temples throb. "I hope he doesn't come to the hospital while I am at work." I huff, realizing there's absolutely nothing I can do at this point that will satisfy my mother. Other than allowing the pond scum to apologize—in person, apparently.

"Well..." Mom hesitates. "I told him you were off today, so he's on his way."

My eye twitches more furiously than a hornet that's been sprayed with hairspray. "You did not!" I manage to force the words through clenched teeth.

"I didn't think it was a good idea for him to drive all the way out there if you wouldn't be able to talk." She sighs. "Really, Karlee, try to be an adult about this."

A sharp knock on the door interrupts my scathing retort. This had better be a newspaper salesman. "Mother, I have to go. We will discuss this more later." I don't even give her a chance to respond before I end the call.

Another rap on the door has my blood pressure climbing. This cannot be happening to me. I peek through the peephole. There he is. Mr. Cheaterpants. In the flesh.

I debate not answering, but a third knock lets me know he's not walking away.

"Karlee, I know you're in there. I saw your SUV in the parking lot." Patrick's nasally voice penetrates the door, making my headache worse.

Swinging open the door, I resist the urge to punch him in his smug face. I don't look good in orange. I repeat the phrase over and over in my head.

"I could have been out with friends, or my boyfriend." I cross my arms over my chest and stand, blocking the doorway. "Presumptuous to assume I'd be home today."

"Oh, come on, Karlee. We both know you only have time in your life for work. Besides, you don't have a boyfriend—your mom would have told me." He rolls his eyes. "Can I come in?"

My mouth drops open. "Come in? To my house? I don't think so. Say what you need to say and leave."

"Don't be like that. I came to apologize for how I ended things. I should have been more sensitive. Honestly, I'm surprised you cared." He shrugs his shoulders, causing his button-up shirt to bunch awkwardly. He never wore the right size clothes.

"You didn't think I'd care?" I ask, disbelief causing my voice to rise. "Unbelievable. I spent six years of my life with you. We had plans, Patrick." I am not letting him turn this around on me.

"Listen, if I can't come in, can we at least go to the coffee shop down the road?" He holds his hands out in surrender. "Please."

I blow out a deep breath, trying to get ahold of myself. "Fine, but I'm meeting you there. You get fifteen minutes of my time. Then I'm leaving."

"Thanks, Karlee. I appreciate it."

"I'll meet you there in ten minutes." I shut the door in his face. I know I should be more mature about this, but I'm not prepared to have this conversation. At all. Maybe I should move again and not give my mom my address. I've never been great with conflict.

I shake my head and grab my keys and purse off the kitchen counter. May as well get this over with.

A few minutes later, I pull open the glass door to the Coffee Loft. The smell of roasting coffee beans hits me and soothes the ache that's building at the base of my neck. Caffeine always helps, or at least it doesn't hurt. Little round tables are situated near bright, open windows, making the space airy and inviting. In the back corner is a rounded sofa-style booth. Cozy.

I make my way to the counter and peruse the menu boards. A selection of seasonal coffees, and local favorites make the list, along with a few donuts and pastries.

"Can I help you?"

I glance down at the barista behind the counter. Her deep coffee brown eyes and pale skin are accented by her blue hair. I stare a second too long, before I get it together. "I'll have an iced latte please, and a blueberry scone."

Lacey, according to the name embroidered on her Coffee Loft apron, smiles. "Not used to seeing blue hair, huh?" She punches my order into the computer.

"No, I'm sorry. It looks great on you, though." I grin sheepishly. I may be having a bad day, but it's no excuse for bad manners.

Lacey laughs. "Thanks, I'm experimenting." She winks at me and gives me my total.

Before I can swipe my card, I hear someone clear their throat behind me. I roll my eyes. Seriously, I couldn't even get my coffee first?

"I'll buy that," Patrick says. "It's the least I can do."

I step back from the counter. He's right, buying a coffee and a scone is the least he can do.

After grabbing my latte and scone, I make my way to an open table near a window. At least I can stare outside.

Patrick slides into the open seat across from me at the small table. "Thanks again for agreeing to meet with me."

I raise an eyebrow in response. "What was so important that you drove all the way to Piney Brook to see me?"

Patrick's eyes dart to his lap. "Cutting right to the chase, huh?"

I don't answer. Instead, I break off a bit of my scone and pop it into my mouth. Heavenly. I'll have to come back here with better company.

"I really am sorry, Karlee." He reaches across the table to take my hand, but I jerk it back and place it in my lap.

"For what?" I ask, unwilling to give him an inch. He wanted this conversation—he can have it.

"You were working so much, and we barely saw each other. It felt like you were already gone from the relationship. When Celine and I started hanging out, I swear it was just as friends. We both missed you. Over time, it became something more." He shrugs his shoulders, his shirt shifting oddly on his body.

I snort. "Hanging out doesn't become something more when you're in love with someone else." Then it hits me—Patrick wasn't in love with me anymore. Tears burn the backs of my eyes, but I refuse to let them fall. "You weren't, were you?" I take a breath and steel my nerves. "You weren't in love with me anymore."

His eyes drop to the table for a moment before finding mine. "I don't know, Karlee." He lets out a deep breath. "Were you really in love with me? Or were we just doing the next thing? Ticking off the boxes?"

I stare at him, prickles of unease making me squirm in my seat. Were we just ticking the boxes? Did I want the happy home—with the mom and dad and two point five kids—so bad that I pushed through even when I didn't love him anymore?

"I..." My voice cracks. I take a sip of my latte and try again. "I really don't know." I answer honestly.

He nods. "I don't think either of us stopped to consider what we wanted more—each other, or the dream. In the end, it was all you could talk about. Saving money, buying a house. It got to be too much. I felt like you wanted the house more than you wanted me."

I rub my temples. This day is giving me whiplash. "So, you cheated on me?" I ask. "Rather than talk to me about how you were feeling, Patrick. You cheated on me with my best friend."

"I know," he says. "I made a mistake."

I laugh. "A mistake? No, Patrick, a mistake is forgetting my birthday. You can't call dating my friend behind my back a 'mistake.'"

"It's not like I meant for it to happen, Karlee. Don't you think you could forgive me? Maybe we could try again?"

I'm shaking my head no before the words even leave my mouth. "Not a chance."

He nods, finally understanding. "I'm still sorry for how things went. I should have broken things off with you officially before things ever moved in that direction. It wasn't intentional. It was just... I didn't feel like *I* mattered to you anymore."

I sigh and take another bite of scone, the chewing giving me time to think. "Okay," I say finally. "I'm not saying what you did was right, but I forgive you. That doesn't mean I want to rekindle our relationship, though."

Patrick's shoulders sag. "I understand. Could we be friends?"

"No," I say honestly. "I don't think that's a good idea."

"What about Keelee's wedding? I could be your date, you know... so you don't have to go alone. As friends."

I sit back in the chair. I'm about to answer, when the door swings open and in walks Evan, looking downright stunning. His clean white t-shirt stretches across his muscular chest, and the jeans he's wearing fit him like a glove. The hairs on my arms stand on end.

"I..."

"Karlee, there you are," Evan says, looking from me to Patrick and back again.

Suddenly, I feel like a kid who's been caught stealing a bubble gum ball from the candy store. "Um, yep. Here I am," I say, standing to make the introductions. "Evan, this is Patrick. Patrick, my..."

"Boyfriend," Evan says sharply. Patrick stands and extends his arm. Evan smiles, taking Patrick's outstretched hand and shaking it a bit too firmly. "Evan."

I squeak, and heat blooms in my face. I look around the nearly deserted coffee shop and realize we are now entertainment for Lacey and her co-worker.

I resist the urge to bury my face in my hands and rush from the building. Barely.

"Nice to meet you, Evan," Patrick says, shock making his eyes wide. "Karlee didn't mention you." He looks at me as though I've hurt his feelings.

"I..." I say, trying to think on my feet.

"It's new," Evan says, placing his hand on my shoulder. "Isn't that right, sunshine?"

At a loss for what else to do, I laugh. Though I'm sure it sounds forced by the way Evan looks at me.

"Well, Karlee. Thanks again for letting me apologize in person." Patrick leans in to kiss me on the cheek, but Evan steps in the way. "Right," Patrick says, stepping back. "I should get going."

I smile and nod from my place behind Evan. "Okay."

"See you around." Patrick gives Evan a little salute and winks at me before turning on his heel and leaving the coffee shop.

I sink into my chair and drop my head between my knees. I feel like I might faint.

"Are you okay?" Evan asks gruffly. "Karlee?"

I mumble something in response, but even I'm not sure what I say.

Evan steps away for a moment and returns with a cool napkin that he drapes across the back of my neck.

"Here's a glass of ice water for your girlfriend," Lacey says, handing Evan a to-go cup of water. "Just so you know, she looked annoyed with that guy the whole time. Ashlan and I were sort of taking bets on whether or not she would throw her iced latte in his face."

I snort and sit back up. "Like I'd waste perfectly good coffee." Wait, she said "girlfriend." My eyes dart to Evan to see if he noticed. "Um, she thinks we're together," I whisper when it appears he didn't hear her.

He shrugs. "I'm sure she does. I did say I was your boyfriend." Evan looks at me like I've grown another head. "Are you feeling okay?"

"What if they tell other people?" I ask, glancing at the girls as they whisper behind the counter.

"Then they tell other people. What's the matter? Are you ashamed of me, Sunshine?" Evan winks at me.

"What?" I ask, confused. "I don't even know what is happening anymore." I wring my hands together frantically. I must have woken up in the twilight zone.

Chapter Ten

Evan

When I walked into the Coffee Loft and spotted Karlee sitting with another man, hot fire burned in my belly. The fact that she looked so uncomfortable only added to the boiling in my gut. I forgot all about my errand to bring Tracey coffee and a donut, and went into protector mode.

Then she introduced the man as Patrick, and I wanted to punch him square in the nose. Who cheats on their girlfriend with her best friend?

"What are we going to do?" Karlee asks, looking at me as though I have all the answers.

I shrug. "Nothing." I have no intention of correcting the baristas behind the bar. That churning feeling in my gut told me not to walk away from this. I've never felt that way before. It makes me wonder if Karlee's it for me.

"What!" she nearly shrieks, breaking me out of my train of thought. "How... but..."

I gently move the wet napkin from her neck to her forehead. "Sit tight for a minute. I'll be right back." Going to the counter, I quickly place my order to-go and pay the bill. When it's ready, I grab the tray of drinks, complete with another iced latte for Karlee, and head back to where she's sitting with a worried crease between her eyes.

"Come with me?" I ask. "Please. We can talk more, away from listening ears." I tilt my head toward the counter where Lacey and Ashlan stand wiping the same section of countertop.

She stares at me a moment before standing. "I think I'll just head home. This has been a crazy day."

"I have coffee," I say, not above bribing her right now. After seeing her so upset, I'm not ready to let her go.

She glances at the to-go tray I'm holding. "Why so many cups?" she asks.

"I'm taking some coffee to my sister and brother-in-law this morning. I'm going to babysit and send her and her husband out for a lunch date. It's been rough since Brody broke his arm and they need a break."

She stares at me for a long moment, metaphorical smoke pouring from her ears at how hard she's thinking. Everything inside me freezes, waiting for her answer.

"I think I need to go home." She looks at her feet. "I'm sorry. Today's been too much for me already."

My heart slams into my chest. "Disappointed" doesn't begin to describe how I'm feeling. "Okay, but I'm going to stop by later with takeout from Beats and Eats. I don't know that you'll feed yourself in this state." *Please don't say no.*

She hesitates a second, but then nods her head. "Okay, thanks."

Together, we walk out the door and to her car.

"Here," I say, handing her one of the cups. "At least take your coffee."

She takes the cup and places it in her center console. "Thanks, Evan. I'll see you later."

I wait until she's pulled away from the curb and heads back towards the apartment before getting everything settled into my truck.

I lean back in the seat and close my eyes. Opening them, I start the truck and hit the button to call my dad as I pull out onto the road.

"Evan. Didn't expect to hear from you today, son." Dad's voice booms in the truck.

"Hey, Dad, I have a question for you. Are you with Mom?" As much as I love my mother, she won't rest until I've put a ring on Karlee's finger if she thinks there is so much as a chance that she might be the one.

"Nah, she went to play bridge down at the church. Why?"

I sigh. "How did you know Mom was the one for you?"

The line goes silent for a moment. "Well, I hate to say it, son, but I just knew. One day I looked at her and everything had changed. She wasn't the cute girl from math class anymore. She was everything." He chuckles. "Convincing her wasn't as easy."

I laugh, imagining him trying to convince eighteen-year-old Mom that she was it for him. "Hard sell?" I ask.

"She came around," he says, joy evident in his voice. "So, any particular reason you're asking?"

I debate telling him no, but he'll find out soon enough. I never was good at keeping secrets, and the wedding we're going to means I'll miss family dinner. "I'm figuring it out," I say, unwilling to give anything more just yet. "I won't make it to family dinner next time, though. A friend needed a plus-one for a wedding, and I agreed to go."

Dad grunts. "A plus-one to a wedding," he says, pausing. "For a friend."

"Yeah," I say, holding my breath, hoping that he won't push it.

"All right, are you telling your mother, or would you like me too?"

I let out the breath in a big whoosh. "I'll call her later and let her know." If he tells her, she'll be calling me anyway. "I just pulled up to Tracey's. I'm going to watch the kids while she and Lawrence go out for a while to take a break."

"That's nice. I'm sure they'll enjoy that."

"I hope so," I say. I know it can't be easy to get adult time with two little kids running around. "Okay, Dad, I'll let you go so I can go in and get mauled. Thanks for the advice. Talk to you soon."

"Evan?" Dad calls. "If you've found her, don't let her go. Louise wasn't it, son. I hope you see that now."

I cough a bit, trying to think of what to say, but Dad hangs up before I do.

Hopping out of the truck, I grab the tray of coffee and head to the front door. Tracey's white ranch-style house sits back from the road a bit, giving her a spacious front yard. Hibiscus bushes line the front of the house, and a small porch leads to the deep green front door.

I knock, careful not to spill the coffee, and wait. I hear a little kid yelling from inside, and laugh. From the sounds of it, a broken arm hasn't slowed down Brody's superhero moves.

The door swings open, and Tracey eyes me warily before noticing the coffee. "You brought the goods, you may enter." She stands back from the door and waves her arm toward the mess. "As you can see, we are making memories. Or something like that."

I laugh at her use of the corny line everyone says once they have kids' toys littering every surface of their home. "Where's Lawrence?"

"Right here." Lawrence pops up from behind couch cushions that are arranged upright in a semicircle on the floor. "Are you good, or evil?" he asks seriously. Brody giggles from behind the cushions.

"I come bearing gifts, and an offer of free babysitting. So, I think that means I'm good." I laugh when he pops to his feet.

"Seriously?"

"Yep. You two go get dressed and get lost for a couple of hours. Uncle Evan has some bad guys to catch." I hand Lawrence the tray of drinks and the bag of donuts and make my way to the fort on the floor. "May I join you in your quest to rid the world of evil?" I ask in my best superhero voice.

Brody giggles. "Yes!"

Tracey takes a big gulp from the coffee cup in her hand and moans. "Have I told you lately you're my favorite brother?"

I laugh. "I'm your only brother."

"Emelia is down for her nap, but she will be up in about forty-five minutes. Then they'll need lunch, and . . ." She pauses and looks at Lawrence. "Nevermind. You've got this."

Lawrence grins at her and ushers her down the hall to their room to change.

"Let's get the bad guys while your sister sleeps. When she gets up, we'll make peanut butter and jelly sandwiches and have a picnic outside. How's that sound?" I ruffle Brody's curls.

"Yeah!" he says before crouching behind the pillows. "Careful, Uncle Evan, there's a bad guy, just came around the corner."

I duck down, just in time, according to Brody, who pops up and vanquishes the bad guy with his sword. A pool noodle that Lawrence cut down and decorated with tape. Smart idea if you ask me.

Several hours later, Brody and Emelia are worn out and resting on a pallet on the living room floor, watching their favorite animated movie when Tracey and Lawrence come in looking refreshed.

"Hey," Tracey says, spying the kids on the floor. "How did it go?"

I point to them and raise an eyebrow. "Good. They're great kids, Trace. They've just got a lot of energy. Nothing wrong with that."

She grins and comes to stand in the living room. "Thanks. We really needed that."

"What are uncles for?" I ask, getting to my feet. "I'm going to get going, though."

"You sure you can't stay for dinner?" Lawrence asks.

"Nah, I've got some things to do tonight. I appreciate the offer." I bend down to tell the kids I'm leaving and notice they've both fallen asleep. Standing back up, I take a moment to soak them both in. Being an uncle is amazing. All the cuddles and fun, without the late-night screaming.

A few minutes later, I'm pulling into the Beats and Eats parking lot. My stomach growls when the smell of hot fries hits my nose. I head to the counter and take a seat. May as well be comfortable while I wait.

"Hey there, Evan," Gabby says, handing me a menu. "What can I get you?"

I hand her back the menu and place our order. Hopefully Karlee is a creature of habit, because I order her what she had the day we picked up her furniture.

"Hey, Gabby?" I pause, while she finishes punching in the order—two burgers, fries, and two chocolate shakes to go.

"Yeah?"

"I know it's none of my business, but what happened with you and Heath?"

Her back stiffens, and the smile drops from her face. "You'll have to ask him." She turns and walks away without a backward glance.

I rub my hand over my face and groan. Maybe I should have left it alone, but clearly they are both still upset.

A few minutes later, Ms. Daisy, the owner, hands me my order. "Here we are," she says, smiling. "Sometimes, when hearts get broken, it's hard to talk about." She nods her head toward Gabby, who is busy rolling silverware in the corner.

"Thanks," I say, taking the bag. "I didn't realize."

Daisy pats my hand. "I know, dear. You take that on to Karlee, and you two have a good night." She winks and walks away.

I grin. It seems the rumor mill has been busy this afternoon. Then I remember how worried Karlee was at the Coffee Loft and the smile drops from my face.

Leaving the diner, I decide now's as good a time as any to tell Mom I won't be at family dinner next time. If I wait too long, Dad will tell her.

Pulling up her name, I hit the dial button and listen to it ring through the car speakers.

"Hello, son."

"Hey, Ma. How are you?"

"Better now that you called," she says.

I love my mom. No matter what happens, she always makes us feel special and loved. I hope I can be like that with my own children one day.

"Thanks, Ma. Listen, I won't be at the family dinner next Sunday."

There's a pause at the other end of the line.

"Why not?" she asks. Family dinners are important to my parents. It was hard on them when Tracey moved out and got married. Even harder when I eventually moved out, too.

"Well . . ." I hesitate, unsure how much to share. "My friend needed a date for her sister's wedding."

"Your friend?" she asks. "Is she a special friend?"

I sigh, resigned to my fate. "She is, Ma. She's very special, but it's new," I say, thinking it's so new Karlee doesn't even know yet. "And I'm still not sure how this will go."

She squeals and calls for my father. "Did you know Evan has a special 'girl' friend?"

I hear my dad's voice mumbling something in the background.

"When can we meet her?" Mom asks. "What's her favorite food? I'll make it for the next family dinner. Should we have an extra one this month since you'll miss this one?"

"Mom . . ."

"Maybe I could talk to Tracey and Lawrence about changing the day, just this once. Since this is such a special occasion."

"Mom!"

"What, dear? You don't need to yell, my goodness."

I laugh. If I didn't love her so much, her excitement would annoy me. "Mom, I think we need to be patient and hold off. I don't want to overwhelm her with too much at once."

Mom huffs. "Evan Christopher Thompson. Are you calling your family too much?"

"No, Ma. I'm not. I'm just saying, let me take her on more than one date before I bring her home to meet the parents."

She sighs, and I know I've upset her. "I'm sorry, Ma. I know you're excited . . ."

"You're right. After the number Louise and her parents pulled on you, I wasn't sure you'd ever date again."

I sigh and grip the wheel harder. "Well . . ."

"I know what her parents said to you at the hospital, Evan," she says, interrupting me. "But you have to know they were hurting and lashing out at anyone they could. They knew full well that accident was her fault for doing it and their fault for not listening to you to begin with."

"But . . ."

"No buts, son. This new friend must be pretty special if she got you to come out of your shell again."

I smile. "She is special, Mom. I think she's it for me, but I have to take it slow. Her ex really hurt her, and I don't want to rush her."

"I understand," Mom says, finally calming down a little. "Can I at least know her name? Is she from Piney Brook? Do I know her?"

I chuckle. "Her name is Karlee. She moved to Piney Brook at the beginning of June, so I doubt you would know her."

"Okay, son. I don't love that you won't be here, but I understand. Call me when you get back from the wedding and we can make plans then."

I shake my head. "Will do. I love you, Ma."

"Love you, too."

I hit the disconnect button just as I pull into the parking lot.

Chapter Eleven

Karlee

My phone dings again. I cringe. How has word spread so quickly? I peek at the message.

Terran: Girl, I KNEW something was going on with the hot neighbor!

Seriously? I groan and tuck the phone under the couch pillow. How in the world are we going to fix this?

I hear footsteps in the hallway and jump up. Rushing to the door, I swing it open just as Evan has his hand raised to knock.

"Well, hello, sunshine," he says. His signature dimple is on display, making me melt a little bit.

"Don't call me sunshine, mister." I stand back so he can come inside.

Placing the takeout bag on the coffee table, he steps back and looks at me. Frowning, he steps closer.

I put out my hand to stop him. "No way. You stay there."

He puts his hands up in surrender. "Okay," he says slowly. "What's wrong?"

I laugh, the sound harsh to my own ears. "What's wrong? What's *wrong*? This whole day is wrong!" I wrap my arms around my middle, hoping to hold myself together. "First, my mom gives Patrick my address. Then he shows up claiming I wasn't in love with him anymore anyway—which is true now that I think about it. But he still cheated on me, and that's wrong no matter how you slice it."

I suck in a breath and continue. "Then you appear and declare you're my boyfriend, and now the women from work are talking about it, apparently. How in the world are we going to fix this?" I take a deep breath and fall into the couch cushions.

"Whoa, slow down." Evan sits beside me. "That's a lot to process for anyone." He opens the bag and places my food in front of me. "Why don't we eat, and then we can talk about all of those things one by one?"

He sounds so calm. How is he not freaking out? "Don't you care that people think we are together?"

He pins me with his chocolate eyes. "To be honest, no."

My mouth drops open in shock. *No?*

With one finger under my chin, he closes my mouth and points to my food. "Eat, or it will get cold." He takes a huge bite of his burger and smiles.

I pick up a fry and run it along the edge of the burger, gathering the condiments that are oozing out the sides, and pop it in my mouth.

He shudders but doesn't say a word. Smart man.

We eat our food in silence, which I appreciate. I need the time to regroup. When I got home earlier, I lay down for a nap hoping that when I woke up, this would all be a bad dream. Unfortunately, I woke up to several texts from co-workers who were not the least bit surprised that Evan and I were dating now. They'd seen the sparks, they said.

I roll my eyes.

Evan stands and collects the empty food containers, taking them to the kitchen and throwing them away. He grabs a cold Coke from the fridge and brings it back to the sofa, popping the tab and taking a drink.

"Can we talk now?" I ask, pouting a bit. I slurp up the last of my chocolate shake.

"Sure." He sets the can on the table in front of him and positions his body towards me. "Let's start at the part where you said you weren't in love with Patrick anymore." He grins.

"Or, we could start at the part where I don't know what to tell people who think we are really dating now."

"Well," he says. "What if we just roll with it?"

"Roll with it?" Is he serious right now?

"Yeah," he says, calmly. "What if we just let it be? At least until we get back from your sister's wedding."

"Just let all of Piney Brook think we are dating?" I ask.

He nods. "Would it be so bad to be my girlfriend?"

I stare at him so long, my eyes get dry from forgetting to blink. "Evan, I'm the quiet girl. The nerdy girl, who would rather stay in than go out. Who has a to-be-read list longer than the average life span. I am not the girl who gets the hottest guy in town." I shake my head. "I don't like people gossiping about me. It's part of why I left Rockdale to begin with."

"Listen, I get it. I do. Being the latest gossip isn't fun. Trust me, I know. Just tell your friends that I jumped in to save you from your ex if you're not comfortable with a relationship right now. They'll understand."

I roll my eyes and chew on my thumbnail. "What about every-one else?"

"What about them? They'll get the hint soon enough." He sighs. "Seriously. Let's just focus on getting through the wedding and then we can talk about the rumors... if they're still making the rounds. Who knows, by then, they may have moved onto something else."

I'm rushing around throwing last minute things into my suitcase. I can't believe today is the day we leave for Keeley's wedding. Evan called me a few minutes ago to let me know he's ready to go. Why is it so much easier for men to pack?

Going over my mental checklist one more time, I slam the suitcase shut and zip it up. Heath is staying at Evan's apartment to watch Peanut and Mittens, so I took Peanut and her things over last night so she could settle in.

I text Evan and let him know I'm ready. Grabbing my purse and my keys off the counter, I wheel my suitcase to the front door. I don't even have the door all the way open when Evan steps out of his apartment looking suave in a pair of crisp dark jeans and a t-shirt.

I stare a moment too long. I'm used to seeing him in his work uniform or worn-down jeans. This cleaned-up version is too much.

"Don't worry," he says, mistaking my perusal as disapproval. "I have something to change into for the rehearsal dinner. I just wanted to be comfortable driving."

I laugh. "You're fine. I plan to change, too." I push the suitcase into the hall and shut my door. Evan grabs the luggage and heads down the stairs while I lock up.

"I'll get this into the truck and we'll be good to go."

I meet him at the truck where he's already loaded our luggage in the back. He opens my door and helps me inside as usual, and I can't help but huff. "I can get my own door, you know."

He gets into the truck and buckles his seat belt. Sliding his sunglasses on, he starts the truck and looks at me. "Ready?" he asks, ignoring my protest.

I take a deep breath and nod. "Yeah, I think I am."

He grins. "Let's go, then."

He pulls out of the parking lot and heads for the highway. He has country music playing softly in the truck, and I know it's for me.

"We can listen to something else," I say, reaching for the knob to change the station.

"Why?"

"I know you don't like country music. You don't have to listen to it for me."

He glances in my direction. "It's growing on me. Leave it."

"Okay," I say, unconvinced. I reach into my tote and pull out my bag of goodies.

"What's that?" Evan asks.

"Snacks," I say, opening the ziplock. "Want some?"

He laughs. "We just got on the road. Did you eat breakfast?"

I scoff. "Why eat breakfast when I can eat snacks? That's the best part of a car ride." I grab a candy rope and take a bite. "Yum."

Evan flips his blinker on, pulling into a fast-food chain. "I would rather eat breakfast first if that's okay with you."

I shrug. "To each his own." I take another bite of the chewy goodness.

Evan pulls the truck to a stop and puts it in park. "Do you mind if we eat inside?"

I look longingly at my treat bag. "Later," I say, caressing it.

Evan laughs. "You take car snacks seriously, I see."

"Of course," I say, closing the bag back up and tucking it into the corner of the floorboard. "Let's go."

Evan rushes around to my side of the truck and helps me out. "Thanks."

Once inside, he orders the egg, bacon, and cheese sandwich with a large coffee. "What do you want?"

I chuckle. "I've got snacks, remember?"

He laughs. "Okay, but it's going to be a long weekend, and I'd hate it if you made yourself sick with candy before we even got there."

I roll my eyes, but order a breakfast sandwich for myself. "Mom would have a fit if I couldn't go to the rehearsal dinner tonight," I tell him as we slide into a booth.

"I can see why that might be a problem," he says, opening his sandwich. "Don't they have to pay per person for those things?"

"Yeah, but it's Scott's family that pays for the rehearsal dinner, I think."

He raises an eyebrow.

"Okay, fine. I know it's rude. I'm going. Wouldn't it be more fun to sneak off and do something else, though?"

"Like what?"

"Paintball, zip lining, base jumping..."

Evan laughs. "I didn't take you for such an adventurous soul."

"I'm not," I sigh. "None of those things sound appealing to me." I take a bite of my sandwich. "Except maybe paintball," I say after I swallow.

He nods. "Good to know. No zipline or base jumping, but paintball is on the table."

After we finish eating, and are back on the road, I turn in my seat a bit to face him. He didn't shave yet this morning, and a bit of scruff lines his strong cheekbones. I like it. I wonder what it feels like to touch.

"What's going through that pretty head of yours?" he asks, glancing at me.

"Nothing," I say innocently. Embarrassed he caught me staring.

"Uh huh." He waits a beat. "I think we missed some pretty vital information in our twenty questions when we first met."

I draw my eyebrows together. "What do you mean?"

"Well, we kept it light and fluffy," he says. "So we skipped some of the more personal stuff."

"Oh. What do you want to know?"

"Well, I know about Patrick and Celine. Is there anyone else I should know about?"

I shake my head. "No, not really. You'll meet Keeley and Scott. My grandparents have flown in from Florida, so you'll meet them too. Of course, you'll meet my mom. Other than that, there's really not anyone else."

"All right," he says, nodding his head. "When is your birthday?"

"October 27th. yours?"

"November 24th."

I make a mental note of that for later. "I know your favorite color, that you have a sister, a niece and nephew. You work in the auto shop with your friends. You like baseball, are a loyal friend, and would rather hurt yourself than let someone down," I say. "What else should I know?"

"When have I hurt myself instead of letting someone down?" he asks.

"Well, you went out with Heath when you clearly didn't want to. You took him home and took care of him, even when you were upset with him." I pause. "You listen to country music for me, even though you hate it."

He's quiet.

"I didn't mean to upset you. It was just an observation." I wring my hands together in my lap.

"No, you're not wrong." He grips the steering wheel. "I don't like to disappoint people."

I nod. "Sometimes it's okay to put yourself first," I remind him.

He glances at me. "Yeah, yeah."

"Okay, why were you so upset with Heath? I know he was tipsy, but he seemed like he was being responsible, for the most part. He had a designated driver and was clearly careful not to get sloppy like some people. There was a girl that same night who got dragged out by her boyfriend."

Evan's face pales. If I hadn't been looking at him, I might have missed it.

"What? What did I say?"

Evan swallows hard, his Adam's apple bobbing up and down in his throat. "That girl, the one who left so drunk? That was Louise."

I gasp. "Louise, your ex-girlfriend?"

He nods.

"Oh, Evan. I didn't know."

"She started drinking at parties in high school. At the time, it seemed like that's what everyone was doing. I was on the baseball team and the coach told us if he caught us drinking—even a little—he'd kick us off the team. So I never touched the stuff." He pauses.

"After a while, she was drinking all the time. Paying our friends' older siblings to buy it for her." He shakes his head. "It was out of control. After we graduated, it got worse. She was drinking almost every day. I tried talking to her parents, but they ignored me."

I reach out and touch his arm. "I'm so sorry."

"That's not even the worst part," he says, taking a deep breath. "One night, I refused to go out with her. She had just turned twenty-one and wanted to go to the Curly Pig and party. I told her I needed to stay home that night. I figured if I didn't drive her, she wouldn't go."

"But she did," I guess.

"Yeah," Evan says sadly. "She did. She got drunk and drove her car into a telephone pole. I rushed to the hospital as soon as I found out. Her parents yelled at me. They told me it was my fault. If I'd been the one to drive her that night, the accident wouldn't have happened."

"Oh, Evan," I say, my heart breaking for him. "That's not fair. It wasn't your fault. You didn't make her go, or drink, or drive."

"I know," he says. "I do, but emotionally, I have a hard time letting it go. Especially when they kicked me out of the hospital and wouldn't let me see her."

"Ouch." I rub his arm. "They were hurting and took it out on you."

He nods. "A few days later, she was released from the hospital and called me to tell me she didn't want to date someone who wasn't there for her." He lets out a sad chuckle.

"That's awful."

"I swore after that I wouldn't get involved again." He looks at me oddly.

I blush. "I'm sorry," I say, unsure what he wants to hear right now.

Slowly, I reach for the radio dial, and turn it to the alternative station I know he likes.

He looks at me and smiles. "We don't have to listen to this, you know."

"I know, but don't change it. It's growing on me."

After three hours in the truck we finally pull up to the little motel in Rockville. I'd decided to get a hotel room instead of staying at the house so there was more room for wedding stuff–and to have my space. Since moving to Piney Brook, I've realized how little personal space we had growing up.

Evan parks the truck in a guest spot, and we head inside to check in.

"Hi, there. How can I help you?" the woman behind the counter asks.

"Yes, we should have two rooms booked for the weekend. Karlee Richards."

The woman taps her bright red fingernails on the keyboard and raises a perfect brow. "Hmm."

Chapter Twelve

Evan

"Did you say two rooms?" she asks.

"Yes," Karlee says slowly. "We were supposed to have two rooms reserved for Friday and Saturday nights."

She looks up at us, a frown marring her perfectly made-up face. "I apologize. We only have one room under that name."

Sensing Karlee is about to lose it, I step forward. "Maybe the other room is under my name. Evan Thompson?"

We wait while she looks at her computer.

"No, I'm sorry. We don't have that name down at all. And there are no other rooms available this weekend. There's a big wedding in town, so we've had a higher than usual booking."

Karlee groans. "I know. It's my sister's wedding."

The front desk clerk gives her a half smile. "I'm sorry this happened, but it does have double beds, and a separate living room. Does that help? It's a suite."

"I'll call my mom. There must have been a mix up when she was reserving rooms," Karlee says, already reaching for her phone.

"Does the living room have a pull-out?" I ask calmly.

"Yes, it does." She nods, looking back and forth between the two of us, clearly wondering why having one room would be a problem.

"Great, we'll take it." I can sleep on a pull-out for a few nights. "Thanks."

After finishing the paperwork, the clerk hands me an envelope with the room keys. "You ready?" I ask Karlee, turning to face her. She is staring into space, clearly overthinking.

"Karlee, shall we go?" I try again.

She shakes her head. "Sorry, I got lost in my own head there."

I smile. Her tendency to get lost in her thoughts is cute. "Are you ready to go check out the room? If it doesn't work, I'll find a room somewhere else."

"No," she says, shaking her head. "The next closest hotel is more than forty minutes away. If this doesn't work, I'll have to squeeze into my mom's. She was relieved when I said we could stay at the hotel. She's already over capacity with my sister and her friends staying there."

"Well, we'll just have to hope this works then, won't we?" I bump her shoulder with mine.

Thankfully, she packs light, so I'm able to get both suitcases at the same time. We step inside the elevator and I push the button to take us up to the third floor.

"Thanks for doing this," she says when the doors slide closed.

"What, sharing a suite? I'm sure there's plenty of room."

"No, coming with me this weekend." She smiles a half smile from across the small space. "It's nice to have you here."

"I'm happy to be here with you, Karlee."

The elevator dings, and we get off. Pulling the luggage behind me, I walk down the long hallway until I find the room and swipe the key. The door clicks and I swing it open.

Inside is a ☒large living space. A pull-out sofa lines one wall, with end tables on either side. A small round dining table and two chairs sit off in a corner near a mini fridge, microwave, and coffee pot. I can't say I'm a fan of the floral wallpaper, but it could be worse.

A large bathroom with a soaker tub is to the left, and through a separate door is the bedroom. Two plush double beds take up most of the space, with a nightstand in between. Thick white comforters and several pillows make the beds look inviting. An armoire stands across the room from the double beds, and a small desk sits beside it.

"What do you think?" I ask after she's inspected the room. "Think we can make it work?"

She nods. "Yes, but you get the bedroom. You're my guest."

I shake my head and plant my hands on my hips. "No way. You take the bedroom. You're the sister of the bride."

She lets out a sarcastic laugh. "What does that have to do with anything?"

"I don't know. It sounded better in my head. Seriously, take the bedroom. I'll be fine out here."

Karlee finally caves and agrees to take the bedroom, so I send her in to take a nap. She has to be exhausted after working last night and only getting a short nap before we left. I told her to nap in the truck, but she refused.

Quietly, I set my bag on the luggage rack I pulled out of the armoire. Opening it up, I pull out the khaki slacks and light blue dress shirt I packed for tonight. Thank goodness for wrinkle-resistant fabric. It doesn't actually look too bad.

I drape it across the back of one of the chairs and grab the room key. May as well make myself useful and find some water and more snacks for the room. I quietly close the door behind me and head down to the lobby.

"Where's the closest store?" I ask the front desk clerk.

"It's about half a mile down the road on the right. You can't miss it," she says, leaning a bit too far forward and being a little too friendly.

"Thanks." I turn on my heel without a backwards glance. That was just rude—she'd seen me come in with Karlee.

An hour later, I open the door to the hotel room, arms loaded with bags—bottled water, coffee pods for the machine, and lots of prepackaged grab-and-go items. I quietly close the door behind me and unload the water and fruit into the fridge.

I check the time. Better wake Karlee up so she has time to get ready. Softly I knock on the door that separates the living room from the bedroom. "Karlee," I call through the door. "It's time to wake up."

I hear her groan. "A few more minutes," she calls.

"Okay, but we have to leave for the rehearsal dinner in an hour."

I hear a loud thunk come from the other side of the door. "You okay?"

My hand goes to the handle, and I debate busting in and checking on her.

"I'm fine," she grouches. "I fell out of the bed."

I laugh. I can't help it.

"Don't laugh, it's not funny," she calls before bursting into laughter herself. "Okay, it's a little funny."

"I'm sorry for laughing," I say, trying to get it together. "Are you okay?"

"Yeah, but I might have a bruise," she says. She swings open the door, rubbing her hand on her backside. "The floor is hard."

I chuckle. "I bet. Take a warm shower—that might help." I steer her into the bathroom. "Wait," I call, moving to the mini fridge. "Take this bottle of water with you."

"When did we get water?" she asks, looking around. "And all the food?"

I look at the pile of items laid out on the little table. "I went shopping," I say nonchalantly.

"I see that." She shakes her head. "Thank you."

I nod. "You're welcome. Now, I need you to either vacate the area or shut your eyes, because I'm going to change clothes to go to a fancy dinner tonight."

She squeaks, grabs a muffin, and ducks into the bathroom.

I find myself still smiling even after the door clicks shut.

The rehearsal dinner is being held at an Italian Bistro. Opening the heavy wooden door, I step back to let Karlee enter first. The aroma of freshly baked bread and tomato sauce fills the air, making my mouth water.

Karlee moves to the host stand, and I take the opportunity to stand close to her, placing my hand on the small of her back.

"Hi there. Two?"

"No, we're here for the rehearsal dinner," Karlee says. She looks beautiful tonight. She's done some sort of twist with her hair, pulling it off her neck and bringing the focus to the light pink pants suit she is wearing. She radiates confidence.

The hostess motions for us to follow her. We step into the dining area, and I'm impressed. Strands of lights strung throughout the space cast a warm glow on the room, making it more romantic than I expected. Small tables adorned with white tablecloths sit in the center of the room. Larger tables line the walls, each with a flameless candle as a centerpiece.

We're led to a room off of the main dining room, and the atmosphere is much the same. The centerpieces in here are bright yellow and orange flowers, and twinkle lights line the room, giving it the same soft glow.

The chatter dies as we step through the doorway. All eyes land on Karlee. She steps closer to me, and I reach down and lace our fingers together, offering her my support.

"Karlee!" a young woman shouts. She looks so much like Karlee I do a double take. "You made it!" She wraps her arms around Karlee and squeezes. I loosen my fingers to let go, but Karlee holds tight.

"Keeley, I told you I'd be here," Karlee says, stepping back and taking her sister in. "You look beautiful."

"Thanks." Keeley blushes. A young man with dark red hair steps to her side.

"Hey, Scott, you look nice," Karlee says.

"Are you going to introduce us?" Scott asks.

"Oh, of course. I'm sorry. Evan, this is my sister Keeley, and her fiancé Scott. This is my friend, Evan."

We say our hellos and are about to find our seats when another woman joins us.

"Hello there, you must be Karlee's new boyfriend." She leans in and gives me an awkward hug.

"Hi, Mom," Karlee says, accepting the hug from her mother. "This is my friend Evan. Evan, my mom, Katherine." I don't miss the emphasis she puts on my friend.

"Nice to meet you, Mrs. Richards."

"It's nice to finally meet you as well," she says. "Let's find you a seat. They'll be bringing out the food soon. We opted for a family style meal tonight."

She ushers us to a small table in the corner already occupied by an older couple. Karlee beams as she takes the seat I pulled out for her.

"Grandma, Grandpa, I'm so glad you could make it. I've missed you."

Her grandma reaches across the table and pats her hand. "It's nice to see you too, dear. It seems a lot has changed since we were here last." She smiles and tilts her head in my direction.

Karlee nods. "Yes, changed for the good. I'd like you to meet my friend, Evan. Evan, this is my grandma and grandpa, Mr. and Mrs. G."

I raise an eyebrow quizzically as I reach across to shake each of their hands. "Nice to meet you both."

Her grandpa laughs. "She has called us Grandma and Grandpa G since she was little. Apparently, Gregorio was too hard for her to say when she was young." He smiles at Karlee. "It stuck."

Laughing, I bump her shoulder with mine. "I see. That's cute."

The server comes and sets a tray piled with food on a stand beside the table. He places the house salad, bread plate, spaghetti with marinara sauce, a bowl of meatballs, and a dish of chicken parmesan on the table. "Can I get you anything else?"

We all shake our heads no, and he leaves us to our dinner.

The conversation flows easily, and I find myself really enjoying getting to know her grandparents. I can see where she picked up her sense of humor. Her grandpa is a hoot.

After the servers clear away the dinner dishes, Scott stands and thanks everyone for coming. The bride and groom exchange small gifts, and hand gifts out to their parents and the best man and maid of honor as the servers bring out the tiramisu for dessert.

All in all, I'd say the evening was a success.

"Are you ready?" Karlee leans over and whispers, her plate of tiramisu long gone.

"Ready when you are," I say, not wanting to rush her.

She pushes her chair out, and walks around the table, placing a kiss on each grandparent's cheek. "We will see you tomorrow," she says. "It's been a long day, and I'm beat."

I follow her as she says her goodbyes, shaking hands and trying to memorize each new name I'm told. Finally, we step out into the balmy night air, and I take a deep breath.

"Sorry," she says, squeezing my hand. "I know that was a lot."

"It was a great night. I enjoyed getting to know your grand-parents. They seem like lovely people."

"They really are," she says, a smile lighting her face.

Back at the hotel, Karlee insists I get the bathroom first. After a quick hot shower, I change into my pajama pants and throw on a t-shirt. "Your turn," I say, opening the door. I drop my dirty clothes on the floor near my suitcase and rub the towel across my hair again before draping it over the chair to dry.

"Thanks," Karlee calls from the bedroom. She steps out, carrying her pajamas in her arms, and smiles. "You were quick."

I laugh. "Take your time."

"I think I'm going to take a bath if you won't need the bathroom for a while."

"It's all yours," I say, turning to the pull-out sofa. I remove the cushions and yank on the mattress to pull it free. It groans, but doesn't budge. I try again, and it finally pops free. I extend the bed and pull out the sheets I found on the top shelf of the armoire in the bedroom. After making the bed, I gently sit down, testing the springs. Not the worst thing I've ever slept on.

I grab my book from the suitcase and settle in to read for a while.

The next thing I know, I'm startled awake by my alarm blaring in my ear.

Chapter Thirteen

Karlee

I HEAR EVAN RUSTLING around in the main room and shove my head under my pillow. Only my sister would opt for a late morning wedding. Squinting, I grab my phone and check the time. Of course it's time to get up.

I push myself to a sitting position and stretch my hands over my head. Thankfully, last night wasn't terrible. Fingers crossed today goes well, too.

Gathering my clothes, I knock on the door between the bedroom and living room. "Are you decent?"

Evan chuckles. "Yep. Come on out, sunshine."

I push the door open and grumble. "Why do you always call me that?"

He raises one eyebrow. "Because you're so cheerful in the morning?"

I roll my eyes. "Clearly. Is it okay if I take the bathroom to get ready?"

Evan doesn't move from his seat at the tiny table. "Of course. I'm just drinking my coffee and checking the news." He holds up his phone.

"There's a TV right there," I say, pointing at the flat screen perched on the shelves.

He doesn't respond, just takes a sip of his coffee, and waves his phone at me again. Whatever.

Walking into the bathroom, I flip on the light and sigh at my reflection. It's going to take a bit of makeup magic and a lot of concealer to get through this day.

Thirty minutes later, I give up. I pull my hair into a braid that curves artfully around my head and down over my shoulder. It will have to do.

"You almost done in there?" Evan calls. "I need to get dressed so I don't make us late."

Taking one last look in the mirror, I smooth down the wine-colored satin dress I bought for the occasion and step out into the main room.

"Wow," Evan says, his eyes wide as saucers. "You look amazing." Twin spots of pink dot his cheeks, and he lets out a long breath.

"Thanks," I say, turning so he can see the full effect.

"You're going to outshine the bride." He grins. "It's a good thing you have a date. Otherwise, you'd never keep the guys away."

I blush.

Evan winks and grabs his clothes, disappearing into the bathroom.

When he comes back out, I almost choke on the water I'm drinking. "Speaking of looking amazing," I say, attempting to get myself together.

Evan looks down at his navy suit. "Thanks. When you said you were wearing a wine-colored dress, I called my mom to find out what I should wear." He rubs his hands down the front of the suit jacket. "This is okay?"

"It's perfect. You look very nice." Understatement of the year there, Karlee.

"We better go," Evan says, sliding on his dress shoes and putting his wallet in his jacket pocket.

I grab the clutch I brought and make sure I have a room key and my lipstick inside. "I'm ready," I say, taking a deep breath and snapping the bag closed.

We step into the hallway, and Evan slips his hand in mine. I look at him and he leans close.

"Humor me?" he whispers.

I raise an eyebrow, but nod. We arrive at the venue a bit early, allowing us plenty of time to get seated. The converted farm where the wedding is being held is stunning. Green fields as far as the eye can see. In front of a rustic-looking barn, rows of chairs are set out along both sides of an aisle runner. As we make our way to our seats at the front of the bridal side, a soft whinny catches my attention.

"Look," Evan says, pointing across the parking area to another field. "Horses."

I watch them for a moment before Evan takes my hand and guides me to our seats. A few moments later, the groom and his best man take their places in front of the arbor decorated with large sunflowers. Soft music plays from speakers discreetly placed around the ceremony area.

The maid of honor makes her way down the aisle. The flower girl follows closely behind her, guarding her flowers from the ring bearer, who is trying to get her to toss them out. She stops and stamps her foot. "These are mine," she says sharply, earning a laugh from everyone who can hear her.

Finally, the music changes, and my grandfather and Keeley come into sight. My breath catches as I take in my little sister. She radiates joy. The perfect bride.

“Still not as beautiful as you,” Evan says, leaning close to my ear and whispering. His breath tickles my neck and I reach for his hand and lace our fingers together, too caught up in the moment to question it.

The ceremony is beautiful, and when the officiant announces Scott and Keeley as husband and wife, the guests erupt in applause. They share a small kiss before turning and walking down the aisle to where the photographer is already waiting to take pictures.

“Come on, you two,” my mom says, motioning us to follow her to where the bride and groom are being posed this way and that.

“I don’t think we should interrupt.” Mom has a tendency to take over during times like these.

“Don’t be silly. Keeley wanted family shots as well.” She grabs my hand and starts pulling me to the group, now mingling around the photographer, awaiting orders. Halfway there, she turns around and calls to Evan. “You too. Come on.”

He hesitates, looking at me for guidance.

“Mom, we’re not even dating. I’m sure Keeley doesn’t want my friend in her photos.” I don’t want to make this any more awkward for Evan than it must already be.

“Nonsense, Karlee,” Keeley calls. “Of course I want him in the photos. If he was special enough for you to bring to my wedding, he may as well be family.”

I can feel myself turning the same deep red as my dress. “What if he’s camera shy?” I ask, trying one last ditch effort to save her the expense of having him removed digitally later.

Evan wraps his arm around my waist, startling me. "It's fine. Whatever the bride wants, the bride gets. Right, Sunshine? Besides, it's not like I plan on going anywhere." He winks, and my mom grins.

I plaster a fake smile on my face and wait until everyone else is distracted. "What was that?" I hiss quietly.

"It's not worth causing a scene and upsetting the bride, right?" He leans close as though he is placing a kiss on my cheek and whispers. "Besides, I didn't think your mom was going to take no for an answer."

Several photos later, we are finally done and making our way inside the barn where the reception is being held. A sweethearts' table is at the front of the room, but the rest is open seating. We find two chairs at a table off the side of the small dance floor and sit.

"Thank you, again." I take a sip of the water already placed at each seat.

"Please, stop thanking me," Evan says, rubbing my back softly. "I'm enjoying myself."

Other couples join us at the table, making small talk and introducing themselves to one another. I do my best to be polite, but small talk isn't my favorite.

After the bride and groom share their first dance, the buffet lines open. Evan takes my hand when our table number is called and guides me to the line.

"This is quite the spread," Evan remarks, taking a plate and adding skewers of grilled shrimp.

"I think Mom said they were hoping to have a little something for everyone. Keeley didn't want to do a sit-down lunch—too formal for a daytime wedding."

Evan nods. "Why did they choose to get married earlier in the day?"

I shrug. "Flight times. They have to be at the airport early this evening. Scott is taking her to Ireland, where he was born, for their honeymoon."

After lunch, the dance floor opens for couples. I watch as my grandparents dance together, just as in love today as they were when they married fifty-five years ago. Grandpa dips Grandma, and she giggles. It brings a smile to my lips. That's the kind of love I want.

Evan stands and holds his hand in my direction. "Dance with me?"

He frowns when I don't immediately take his hand. "Oh, she doesn't dance," someone calls from across the table.

Evan raises a brow in challenge. "She's danced with me before," he says, reminding me of that night at the Curly Pig.

I stand and take his hand. "I'd love to."

Evan guides me to the dance floor and places his hands at the small of my back, and I wrap my arms around his neck. "Thank you," he says, chuckling softly.

I glance at my sister dancing with her new husband, and smile. "I think they are having a good time."

Evan turns us so he can see them, too. "I agree." He spins me before pulling me close again. "Though they're not the only ones." His eyes on mine leave no room to wonder who he's talking about.

"I am having a nice time," I say, leaning into his touch.

Evan pulls me just a little closer, and when the song ends, I'm not quite ready to leave the dance floor. The Dj announces it's time to cut the cake, though, so we head back to our seats.

Evan places his hand on the back of my chair. I lean into Evan's side and place my head on his shoulder. I wonder what it would be like to be loved by him.

"Karlee, are you almost ready? Checkout is in twenty minutes."

"Almost," I call, stuffing the last few items in my suitcase. After the wedding yesterday, my mother insisted we all go back to her house for dinner. Thankfully, it ended up just being my mom, my grandparents, and Evan and me. Everyone was exhausted from the wedding events, so it wasn't odd when Evan and I left just after we ate. I love my family, but weddings seem to invite people to ask too many personal questions.

Evan is waiting patiently at the small table, his suitcase already by the door, when I come into the main room.

"I'm ready."

"Do you want to stop by your mom's on the way out?"

Mom had mentioned grabbing lunch today, but I told her I had to get back for work. She doesn't have to know I have tonight off. This weekend has been a lot, and I would rather have the time to decompress.

"No. Thanks, though. I told her I was working tonight."

Evan laughs. "Well, that's one way to get out of another meal with the family."

Taking both suitcases, he wheels them down to the front desk and checks us out.

"Did you get a receipt?" I ask, knowing they'd charge my card already on file.

"No, I forgot," he says, guiding me into the parking lot.

"I should go back in and get one." I turn to walk back inside, and he catches my arm.

"Karlee, I got it. It's no big deal."

My mouth drops open. "No, no way. You came here for me. The least I can do is pay for the room."

"It's already done. Please, let me pay?" He puts the suitcases in the bed of the truck and opens my door. "Now let's get you home so you're not late to work." He winks.

"You're terrible," I say, climbing inside the truck.

"Ah, but you still like me."

I blush. He's not wrong. This weekend has been lovely. Holding his hand, feeling like I'm the center of his attention. It's been nice. Too nice. I have to remember he's a friend. He is only doing me a favor, nothing more.

We're half-way home when my phone alerts me I have a text.

Mona: How was the wedding? Did you two scoot off and elope?

Karlee: I told you, he was just pretending to be my boyfriend to get Patrick to leave me alone.

Mona: I wouldn't be so sure about that.

I glance at Evan. He's smiling and humming along to the country song that's playing in the background.

"Evan, we should talk." I realize how ominous that probably sounds and rush to clarify. "I mean, about the rumors back home."

He glances at me and smiles. "What about them? They've died down, right?"

I shake my head and hold up my phone. "Not if the message I got from Mona just now is any indication."

He laughs.

"Don't laugh, I'm serious. What are we going to do? I tried telling them you were only faking it to help me save face, but they're not buying it."

He laughs. "Well, we could always tell people you realized you were still in love with your ex." He shrugs. "Or, we could really give it a shot." A faint pink colors his cheeks.

"Wait, what?"

He looks at me, his brown eyes sparkling. "I like you, Karlee. Why not?"

"Because you don't date, for one," I say, holding up a finger. "Because you don't *like me* like me." I flip up another finger. "The list goes on, Evan."

I don't understand what's happening in my life. One day, I was working toward a goal. Ticking boxes, adding to a hefty savings account, and dreaming of the typical family life. Now I'm in a new city, alone, with possibly the cutest and nicest guy I've ever met offering to what? Pity-date me?

"Who says I don't *like you* like you?" He reaches over and takes my hand in his, giving it a little squeeze before letting go to drive. "Seriously, Karlee, I really like you. I've been drawn to you since the day Peanut ran up that tree."

I suck in a breath. "You have?"

He nods. "Yeah, I even told Heath you were off-limits."

"You did?" I feel like I should have a bigger vocabulary than this right now, but I don't. Words have escaped me.

"I did. When I saw you with Patrick that day at the coffee shop, I—Well, I didn't like that feeling. I wanted it to be me sitting across from you. Except you'd be smiling. I hated how upset you looked." He glances at me from the driver's seat. "What do you say? Give me a chance to woo you?"

I laugh. "Who says 'woo' anymore?"

He grins, that dimple popping out again. "You're right, but you know what I mean. Let me take you on a date. If you don't feel anything for me at the end of the night, we'll figure out a way to tell everyone we're just friends." He looks at me for a long moment. "We are friends, right?"

I sigh. "Okay," I agree. "One date to see how it goes."

He grabs my hand and brings it to his mouth, placing a soft kiss on the back of my hand. "Thanks, Karlee. You won't regret it."

Goosebumps erupt on my arms. I can still feel where his lips, soft but firm, were on my hand, and I wonder what they'd feel like pressed against mine. I feel the bloom of a blush heat my cheeks. "Okay," I whisper.

"When are you off again?"

"Wednesday, but that's a workday for you. We can wait until I have another weekend day off," I protest, not wanting him to go out of his way.

"And when is that?" he asks.

"In two weeks."

"No way. I can't wait that long now that I've gotten you to agree to a date." He seems so eager, and it's endearing.

"Okay, Wednesday it is then." Butterflies do the conga in my chest. I'm nervous, but not because I think the date will be awful. On the contrary. I'm nervous because I'm almost certain it will be the best date of my life.

Wednesday afternoon, I'm staring at the clothes laid out on my bed. I grab my phone and stare at the text message from Evan I'd gotten earlier today.

Evan: Dress comfortably. I'm wearing khaki's and a button-up, if that helps. I'll pick you up at six.

Comfortably. I eye the assortment strewn across my bed. Overwhelmed, I decide to ask for help. I open the text app on my phone and start a group chat. Since the girls at work found out I was going on a real date with Evan, they've been insistent on being there for me. It's kind of nice to have girlfriends again.

Karlee: What do you wear on a casual date when you don't know what you're doing?

I snap a photo of my bed and send it.

Terran: Oh, this is fun! Did he give you any clues?

Karlee: No. Just said to dress comfortably and be ready at five thirty.

I glance at the clock and my heart rate kicks up. It's already four forty-five.

Mona: Wear the sundress. It's casual but flirty. *winking emoji*

Marla: Agree

Terran: I was going to suggest the jeans with the tank top, but they're probably right.

I shoot off a quick text, telling them all thanks, and grab the sundress off the bed.

Thirty minutes later, I'm dressed, my hair is curled, and I've added just a touch of makeup. Casual, but flirty. I like it.

I still have fifteen minutes, so I snap a selfie and send it to the group text. All three women respond right away, telling me it's perfect. Good.

All too soon, there's a knock at the door. I take a deep breath, and slide on my strappy sandals. Closing my eyes, I remind myself taking chances isn't a mistake. I swing open the door, and my jaw drops.

"Sunshine, you look amazing." Evan leans in and places a small kiss on my cheek. "These are for you." He holds out the biggest bouquet of Gerbera daisies I've ever seen. The colorful arrangement is wrapped in white ribbon.

"Thank you," I say, taking the flowers and stepping back so he can come in. "Let me get these in some water, and I'll be ready to go." My eyes drink him in. Charcoal gray dress pants have replaced his usual jeans. A white button-down shirt, with the sleeves rolled half-way up his forearms, accentuates his natural tan. He was handsome at the wedding, but this is next level. He's dressed like this for me.

I turn quickly and head to the kitchen to find the vase I have tucked in the cabinet. When I'm sure he can't see, I wipe around my mouth, making sure I didn't accidentally drool.

"These are beautiful," I say as I fill the vase with water and slide the stems inside. "I love them."

"I'm glad you like them."

I am met with his signature dimpled smile when I turn back around. Placing the flowers on the countertop, I wipe my hands on a kitchen towel and try to catch my breath.

"Ready to go?" Evan leans on the wall near the door, his hands in his pockets.

I pick up the small handbag from the coffee table and nod. "Ready as I'll ever be." I hope my voice sounds steady, because nerves are making my body tremble.

Evan opens the door and lets me out first. I lock the door and drop my keys into my purse. He takes my hand, never dropping it as we descend the stairs, making sure he's one step ahead of me.

"Why are you going ahead of me? There's room for us to go down together." It seems unusual to me.

Evan smiles. "It's proper etiquette for me to go first. That way, if you trip, I can catch you." He winks.

"Oh, really? How do you know that?" I ask, fighting back a laugh.

"My mom made sure I took etiquette classes in high school. She wanted me to be the perfect gentleman." He blushes, and it's the most adorable thing I've seen all day.

"That's really sweet."

He grins. "You'll have to tell her that when you meet her. She'll be thrilled her efforts paid off, and I'll get some brownie points."

We both burst out in laughter. "A momma's boy, huh?"

He shrugs. "A family guy, really."

When we get to the bottom of the stairs, he lets me lead the way to his truck, but when I put my hand on the door handle to open the door, he stops me.

"I'll get that." He looks at me with his deep brown eyes. "Okay?"

I shrug. "Okay, but I am capable of opening a door, you know."

Evan opens the door and gives me a hand up. "I know, but I enjoy taking care of you a bit."

Before I can respond, he shuts the door and walks to his side of the truck. Other guys I know only open doors because they feel obligated to. This feels different—like he's choosing me.

Chapter Fourteen

Evan

I'M ON MY WAY to work, thinking about Karlee and our date later, when my phone rings through the car speakers. I glance at the display. Mom. I laugh to myself and hit answer. I'm surprised she waited this long.

"Hey, Mom. Is something wrong?" I ask, knowing full well she just wants to be nosey. Some people might find that too much, but I know her heart is in the right place. Besides, she's been like this my whole life.

"No, can't I just want to call my son to tell him to have a nice day?" She feigns offense, but I can hear dad laughing in the background.

"Of course," I say, about to call her bluff.

"I hope you have a nice day, son."

"Well, if that's all, I've got to run. Have a nice day, Ma."

"Wait," she calls, finally unable to contain herself. "Did you have a nice time at the wedding?"

I burst out laughing. "So that's why you called at eight in the morning," I say, still chuckling a bit.

"Well," she says, finally giving up her pretense. "Did you? You never called me when you got back. How am I supposed to know? Besides, you said we could meet her after the wedding."

"Leave the boy alone, Marge. He's on his way to work for goodness' sake," Dad says from somewhere nearby.

"Yes. I did," I say, cutting her some slack. "We had a great time together. In fact, you'll be pleased to hear I'm taking her on a date tonight."

She squeals so loudly I reach for the volume to turn it down.

"Evan, where are you taking her? What are you wearing?"

"I've got this, Mom. Thanks, though," I say, glad the news of the date has distracted her from pushing to meet Karlee. I can't wait to introduce her to my family, but I don't want to overwhelm her either. And let's face it, Mom can be a lot.

"Okay, fine," Mom says. "Don't forget to bring her flowers. She deserves flowers."

I laugh again. "Mom, you don't even know her. How do you know she deserves flowers?"

"She caught your eye, she deserves the flowers, Evan. And not roses, everyone does roses. Something unique."

"All right, Mom, I won't forget the flowers."

"And you will wear something other than jeans?"

I sigh. "Yes, Ma. I'll wear something other than jeans, and I'll get her flowers."

"But not roses," she reminds me.

"Not roses," I agree, shaking my head.

"Good boy," she says, pleased with herself. "I can't wait to meet her."

I smile. I can't wait for her to meet my family either.

I'm pulling into the parking lot at work when my phone rings again. I sigh. That was fast.

"Hello."

"Hey, little brother," Tracey says tauntingly. "What's this I hear about a date tonight?"

I sigh. "I just got to work. I don't have time to get into it."

"Fine, meet me for lunch at the mall and I'll help you pick out an outfit."

"Tracey, I don't have enough time to go to the mall on my lunch break. Good grief."

She sighs. "Okay, we'll go to the men's clothing store down the road from Beats and Eats. You can buy me lunch, and I can pick out your clothes."

I laugh. "Fine, I'll meet you at Beats and Eats for lunch. I'll even pay, but I'm picking out my own clothes."

I hear her start to argue, and cut her off. "Got to go. See you later."

I hang up and shake my head. What have I gotten myself into?

I almost drop the flowers when Karlee opens the door. She's always beautiful, but this look takes my breath away. Her soft brown hair hangs in loose curls around her shoulders. I want to reach out and run my fingers through it to see if it's as soft as it looks. The sundress she chose hits her just below the knee, and the muted yellow color looks good against her tanned skin. Little white daisies dot the dress, making me glad I chose a daisy arrangement.

"Have I mentioned how beautiful you are?" I ask, unable to keep quiet anymore.

She smiles, and my heart flutters.

"Thank you. You look nice as well."

"Thanks," I grin. There's no way I'm telling her I went and bought this outfit on my lunch break. Tracey was right. When I walked into the store I realized I didn't own anything nearly nice enough for tonight. I want to pull out all the stops. To really woo her. I may have given my mom a hard time on the phone, but this date with Karlee is important to me.

I help her into the truck and rush to my door. I have the radio set to her favorite country station. It's a sacrifice, but if it brings a smile to her face, it's worth it.

I tap my fingers on the steering wheel, keeping time with the beat of the music. She's humming along softly, tapping her feet on the floorboard. I could see her like this, riding shotgun, next to me forever. It should scare me, but it doesn't.

"So, any guesses about our date?" I was careful not to give any hints, but I'm curious what she likes.

"I'm guessing we aren't skydiving," she says, grinning.

I shake my head no.

"Rock climbing's probably out." She purses her lips and tilts her head. "Are we hiding a dead body?"

I burst out laughing. "What?"

She shrugs. "I noticed a bag in the back."

I glance at her and smile. "No. No dead bodies will be hidden today."

She wipes her hand across her forehead. "Phew, that would have been an awkward first date."

"You really don't have any reasonable guesses?" I ask. I love her sense of humor, but I'm surprised she didn't have anything in mind. It would have driven me crazy not to know what the plan was.

"Well," she hesitates. "I'm not really sure. You've already passed Beats and Eats, so I am guessing that's not where we're headed."

"No, not for our first date."

She glances around. "I don't really know. Where do people go on dates in Piney Brook?"

I laugh. "Usually Beats and Eats or the Curly Pig." Her eyebrows shoot up and I laugh harder. "Don't worry, we're not going to the Curly Pig either."

She laughs. "Good. Don't get me wrong, I enjoy a night out, but it's just not my scene. I'd rather go see a movie or something."

I glance at her. "Then why were you there that night?" I ask curiously.

"The girls from work invited me. I'm trying to make some new friends in town, so I agreed." She smiles and tucks a strand of hair behind her ears. "Can't say I regret going. I ended up having more fun than I expected."

I grin, hoping she's talking about running into me. "Me too." I was annoyed at bumping into Louise, and Heath went a little more overboard than I'd like, but it was the first time I'd seen Karlee socially. It had been nice to see that side of her.

I pull onto the dirt road that leads up the mountain and slow down. No sense in bumping us all around. There's a lookout near the top where you can park. It's got a great view out over the valley. It's not a fancy restaurant, but I'm hoping she likes it.

I got the idea from the internet, honestly. Along with what to bring for dinner. I was racking my brain to come up with something different to do for our first date. I didn't want to take her to the usual places. That's where you take your highschool crush, or your college girlfriend, not someone you're trying to impress.

She looks around curiously as we climb higher up this deserted road, and I realize that she might be a little creeped out. "Don't worry, we're almost there. I promise I'm not taking you to the middle of nowhere and leaving you." I grin as she lets out a deep breath. "There's a spot up the mountain I want to show you. I promise it will be worth it."

"I trust you," she says after a moment.

My heart threatens to burst out of my chest. I know that took a lot for her to say. She doesn't seem to trust easily after Patrick hurt her. I won't take that lightly. "I trust you, too."

I back the truck into the parking spot of the overlook and turn it off. "Here we are."

She looks out the window, confusion causing her eyebrows to scrunch and giving me a glimpse of what a much younger Karlee must have looked like. It's cute. I wonder if her kids will have that same expression. I shake that thought free. Too soon to be thinking along those lines.

"I packed us a picnic dinner, and I've got blankets in the back of the truck. I figured we could get comfortable, eat and talk, and watch the sunset." I rub my hand across the base of my neck. Maybe this was a horrible idea. She'd probably like something more sophisticated, like dinner at the local lodge. "The view from up here is amazing. If you'd rather not, we can go back into town and have dinner at Beats and Eats," I offer, suddenly self-conscious.

She grins. "This sounds wonderful. I haven't explored the mountains around here yet."

Relieved, I smile back. "Don't open your door, I'll come get it." I wait for her to nod before hopping out of the truck.

I never really enjoyed doing these little things for Louise. She always made a big spectacle of the fact that I was a gentleman. I think she liked the attention from her friends. Karlee couldn't be more different, preferring to stay out of the spotlight. I tuck that away to think about later. Now's not the time to dwell on old memories.

Once I've helped Karlee out of the truck, I go around and lower the tailgate. Finding the bag that I stowed the blankets in, I unzip it and arrange them so we'll be comfortable. I should have brought cushions or something to make it softer for her. Next time. If there is a next time. I already hope there is.

"Can I help?" Karlee asks, standing to the side.

"Nope, almost done." I put the last blanket in place and grab the picnic basket from behind my seat in the truck. Once it's in the truck bed, I help Karlee climb up, looking away when her dress inches up the backs of her thighs just a bit.

"Sorry," she says, slapping a hand down to keep the dress from climbing any further.

I climb up into the truck bed and settle in beside her. "It's okay," I say, bumping her shoulder. "I looked away." I wink when she blushes a soft pink.

"I appreciate that, but I have shorts on underneath, just in case."

"I hope you're hungry," I say as she lifts the lid of the picnic basket to peek inside.

"What are we eating?"

Taking the lid all the way off, I reach inside and start setting containers out. "I wasn't sure what you like, so I got a few options." Passing her a plate, and a bundle of silverware wrapped in a napkin—thank you, internet—I start naming the dishes.

"I got chilled fried chicken strips, salad with a vinaigrette dressing," I say, holding up the small bottle of salad dressing. "A fruit salad, some potato salad, turkey and cheese with crackers, and some sparkling grape juice since neither of us really drink. I also have water if you don't like the juice."

Her eyes are big as she takes in all the choices. "That's a lot of food," she says, eyeing me warily. "We won't be able to eat all of this."

I wave my hand over my stomach. "You'd be surprised," I say. "Ask Liam. He was shocked by how much I can eat."

She tilts her head to the side. "Who's Liam?"

I stop adding food to my plate and grin. "I forget sometimes you're new in town and don't already know everyone. Liam is my buddy Brant's stepson. He and Morgan got married this past spring. Then there's Daniel. He has a daughter named Elli. She's a hoot. A ball of energy that never stops. He finally got brave and convinced his girlfriend Reese to give them a chance. It was touch and go there for a week or so, but they patched it up on the Fourth of July, and have been inseparable since. And you've already met Heath."

"Wow," she says, tucking her hands under her legs. "You have a close group of friends."

I nod. "We are a pretty tight-knit group."

She picks up her fork and takes a bite of her salad. "I didn't really make time for friendships back home. I had been working so hard to put away money for a wedding and a house that I didn't see how I'd shut everyone out."

I take her free hand in mine and give it a squeeze. "Sometimes we lose sight of what's important. Close ourselves off. It happens. Don't be hard on yourself."

She closes her eyes and bows her head. "That's good advice."

We eat our food in comfortable silence. It's nice. Just existing with her. No pressure to fill in the quiet. The sound of birds calling to each other across the valley provides the background music for our meal.

Once we've finished eating, I pack all the containers back into the picnic basket, making sure the ice packs are in place to keep the leftovers cool. I can eat those for lunch this week.

"That was delicious. Thank you." Karlee leans back on her elbows. "It's so pretty up here. Peaceful."

The sun has started to set and the fiery orange and yellow swirl through the blue of the sky. "It is. It's one of my favorite spots to come and just think."

"I can see why." She crosses her legs at the ankle and grins. "Mind if I steal it?"

"Be my guest." I look out over the valley and watch quietly as the sun sinks a bit lower in the sky causing it to turn purple and pink. The lights from houses along the mountainside and in the valley are starting to flick on, lighting up the semi darkness.

The sun is just about gone when I pull out some camping lanterns I brought and turn them on. I set a few along the edge of the truck bed and a few more on the ground behind the truck. Leaning inside the truck, I turn the key halfway and turn up the volume on the radio. I leave the door open, allowing the music to filter into the night air.

I go back to the bed of the truck where Karlee is sitting with her legs crossed, her sundress tucked down around her knees. "Dance with me?" I ask, holding out my hand. "I've wanted to dance with you again ever since the wedding."

Karlee grins and scoots down the bed of the truck.

"I thought you'd never ask," she says as she takes my hand.

I help her down and pull her closer. There, under the starry night sky, we dance. My hands on her lower back, hers on my shoulders. Swaying to the soft music coming from the truck speakers. It's perfect. She's perfect.

She lays her head on my chest, and suddenly everything clicks into place. I want this. With her. Forever.

Chapter Fifteen

Karlee

Walking into work Thursday evening, I feel like I'm floating on air. I've never had a date like that. After we danced beneath the stars for a while, I suggested we wrap it up. It was getting late, and he had to work this morning.

He helped me back into the truck, packed up the blankets, and took me home. I smile and rub my fingers on my cheek where I can still feel his kiss from my doorstep last night.

I'm still smiling when I slip behind the nurse's station and drop my bags and water bottle on the counter.

"Whoa," Mona says, grinning like the Cheshire cat. "I take it the date went well?" She wiggles her eyebrows up and down.

I laugh at her antics and nod. "It was amazing."

"Well, spill it," Terran says as she makes her way around the counter from a patient's room. "We have a few minutes before the official shift change."

"He was so romantic. He brought me flowers, took me to a lookout where we ate a picnic he'd packed for us, and then we slow-danced under the stars." Butterflies fight for space in my chest. "It was perfect."

"You're making that up," Mona says, a dreamy look on her face. "Guys don't plan dates like that."

I press my hands over my heart and grin. "Mine does."

Mona and Terran wear identical shocked expressions. "So, it's true! You guys are a thing!" Mona says excitedly.

"I think so," I say, uncertainty making it more a question than a statement. "I mean, he said he wanted a chance to woo me."

Terran grins. "So, are you two exclusive, then?"

I pause, worry niggling at my gut. "Well, we didn't officially decide on terms..."

Mona waves her hand in dismissal. "Did you see the way he looked at her at the Curly Pig? He's exclusive. Plus, when have you ever heard of Evan Thompson dating more than one woman?"

Terran raises an eyebrow and nods. "You're right. Never. He's always all in, even if the other person isn't." She rolls her eyes and scowls.

I want to ask what she means, but I don't.

"All right ladies, enough gossiping," Marla says, tucking her purse away. "Give us the report and get out of here so we can do our work."

Mona laughs. "You just want us to leave so you can get the exclusive scoop."

Marla glares at her a moment, but then laughs too. "Report, ladies."

It's after 8:00 a.m. when I finally climb the stairs to my apartment. I'm bone tired. Turns out we were too busy with admissions last night to get a moment to do more than scarf down some food, let alone chat about my date.

I make it to the top, my keys in my hand, and stop. Taped to my door is a note with my name written in big letters.

Adrenaline wipes the fatigue away as I take the note carefully off the door, unlock it, and step inside. Once I've locked the door back, and taken off my shoes, I drop my purse onto the coffee table, and slump down onto the sofa. Carefully, I open the note, and my breath catches in my throat.

Karlee,

Thank you for last night. It was the best date I've ever had.

From the first moment I saw you, with your hair in a messy bun, frantically chasing Peanut, my heart has been drawn to you. I didn't recognize it right away, but you've captivated me. Your smile is like a ray of sunshine, bringing light into my world. It's why I call you Sunshine.

Dancing with you in my arms last night felt so right. As we swayed to the music beneath the stars, it felt like the world disappeared and it was just the two of us.

I know I asked for one date, but I'd be lying if I said I didn't want more. I hope you feel the same way. What do you say, Karlee? Take a chance with me?

Xo

Evan

I hold the letter to my chest, tears slide down my cheeks. I read it again before carefully folding it back and sliding it into my nightstand drawer for safekeeping.

I pick up my phone to text him, but that feels so inadequate after finding his note taped to my door. Deciding I'll wait until I see him this afternoon, I take a shower and slide into my bed for some much needed rest. I have a feeling I'll be dreaming of Evan holding me close while we dance.

I wake up later than usual and have to rush to get ready for work. Peanut is meowing at me furiously from his seat beside his food bowl. I missed feeding time. I slide both legs into my scrubs pants and pull the top over my head before grabbing his bowls and filling them with fresh water and his dinner.

"There you go, Peanut," I say, patting his head as he digs into his dinner.

I rush to the bathroom, pull my hair into a bun, brush my teeth and splash water on my face. Taking a look at myself in the mirror, I cringe. I have sleep lines on the side of my face, and I could have used a bit of makeup today. Oh well, it will have to do.

I grab my purse and keys. I'll have to grab something from the cafeteria later. Gross.

I step outside, and shut the door, quickly locking it and moving toward the top of the stairs. I pause when I see Evan's door. Shoot. I meant to stop by earlier and thank him personally for his note. I glance at my watch and sigh. It will have to wait.

I barely clock in on time, making Mona and Terran raise their eyebrows in question. I'm never late. Never even this close to being late.

"Sorry, I overslept."

Mona and Terran share a look, but don't say anything else.

"Okay, I'm ready." I listen as they give a report, nodding. It looks like another busy night. Great.

I get a short break between tasks and grab my phone.

Karlee: Thank you for the sweet note. I am so sorry. Was going to stop by before work but was running late.

Evan: No worries. I'm glad you got the note. Did you get dinner?

Karlee: No, I'll have to grab something from the cafe vending later.

A patient's buzzer goes off, so I shove the phone back into my bag and get back to work.

An hour later, I'm at the nurse's station, entering notes into the computer when I hear someone clear their throat. I look up and gasp.

"Evan, what are you doing here?" I jump up and go around the counter to where he stands and give him a hug. I step back, reluctant to let him go.

He holds up a bag from Beats and Eats. "You said you didn't have time to get dinner, and when I texted you back, you didn't respond. I figured you were going to be too busy to stop and get food, so I brought you some."

He puts the bag on the counter and tucks his hands into his pockets. "I hope that's okay."

I grab the bag and drop it on the desk behind the counter. "Not just okay. It's perfect. Thanks."

"I got you something different this time. I wasn't sure what you'd want, but I figured probably something lighter than a burger."

I raise my eyebrow in question. "I'm sure it will be delicious. I haven't had anything from Beats and Eats I didn't like."

He smiles. "Well, I'm going to go. I know you're busy. I just wanted to make sure you ate."

I step into his space, wrapping my arms around his middle and soaking him in. "Thank you, Evan. I really appreciate this."

After a beat, he wraps his arms around me and buries his face in my hair. "You're welcome."

I lean back, still supported by his arms, and smile. "Your note was sweet. Is it okay to tell you I think I'd like more dates, too?"

His face lights up, and he leans close to my ear. "You can tell me anything, sunshine." He places a soft kiss on my cheek and steps back. "I'll see you soon." He winks and walks back down the hallway to the elevators.

"Oh my." The radiology tech is standing behind a wheelchair with a silly grin on her face. "I just came up to get 409 B for her X-ray."

I stare at her. "Okay . . ."

"That was so sweet." She sighs. "I wish my boyfriend brought me dinner when I was busy."

I look down the hallway to where Evan was just standing. "He's one of a kind. That's for sure."

She nods her head in agreement. "Definitely. Don't let that one go." She pushes the wheelchair around the corner to collect her patient, leaving me standing in the hallway with my thoughts.

I finally get time to sit down and eat the meal Evan brought me. I pop open the container and grin. A turkey sandwich and a cup of fresh fruit. Perfect.

I pick up my phone and snap a picture. Adding it to the text thread I have with Evan, I add a little message and hit send.

I've just eaten the last bite when a message notification dings.

Evan: I'm glad you found time to eat. *smiley face emoji*

I put the phone back in my bag and smile to myself. Giving Evan a chance might just be the best decision I've ever made.

Friday morning, I roll over and groan. I'm exhausted, and I don't get a day off until Sunday. I've got a plan today, though. And I don't want to run out of time.

Throwing my legs over the bed, I force myself to stand. I stretch my back and yawn. After getting through my morning routine, I head to the kitchen.

Evan's been so great, doing nice things for me even before we were dating. I want to do something nice for him.

Homemade cookies should do the trick. An hour later, my apartment smells like warm sugar and chocolate. Hopefully, he likes chocolate chip cookies. I check to make sure they have cooled and add them to a container.

Grabbing my keys, I head to my SUV and hop in. It doesn't take long for me to find Brant's Automotive Shop. I pull into the gravel lot and into a parking space near the customer entrance.

Stepping out of the SUV with the container in hand, I shut the door and turn toward the building. Evan is already headed in my direction. He looks handsome in his blue work uniform.

I meet him near the door to the lobby. He leans in toward me and kisses my cheek.

"Karlee, I didn't expect to see you here." He grins, giving me a glimpse of that dimple I love so much.

"I wanted to surprise you," I say, holding out the container of cookies. "I hope you like chocolate chip cookies."

He laughs and pulls the container closer to him. "Don't say that too loud. Brant will try and take some from me."

I laugh. "I made two dozen, so there's probably enough to share."

He shakes his head. "Nope, these are all mine. You didn't have to do that, you know."

"I know, I wanted to." I wave at the two men peeking around the corner of the bay doorway at us. "You've been so nice to me since I moved here, and I've not done nearly enough in return."

He frowns. "It's not a competition. I don't do nice things for you so that you'll do something for me."

I look down. "I know," I say finally. "I just don't want you to feel like I'm not appreciative."

"Oh, Sunshine." He sighs and pulls me into a side hug, careful not to get his dirty clothes on me. "I do things for you because I enjoy doing them." He lets me go. "I tell you what. You stop feeling like you owe me, and I promise I'll tell you if I ever start feeling like you're taking advantage of me." He sticks out his hand. "Deal?"

"Deal," I say, and we shake on it. "Now, why don't you introduce me to the two guys who are about to break their necks peeking at us."

Chapter Sixteen

Evan

I turn around quickly, and Brant and Daniel scramble to get out of sight. I laugh and grab Karlee's hand. "Come on, come meet the guys."

I take her inside the shop, careful to keep her out of the messy areas. Brant and Daniel lean over the hood of the nearest car, acting like they are deep in a discussion.

"Give it up, you two. We already saw you."

Brant stands and grins. "Sorry, we were just curious about the woman who has Evan all tied up in knots."

Karlee looks at me and smirks. "Really? Tell me more."

Daniel laughs. "I can see why he likes you."

"Thanks, I think." Karlee laughs, and the sound is music to my ears.

"Brant, Daniel, this is Karlee. Karlee, these two knuckleheads are my co-workers and friends, Brant and Daniel."

"Nice to meet you, finally," Karlee says, shaking both of their hands. "Brant, you have a son, Liam, right?"

Brant nods. "Sure do." He pulls his wallet from his back pocket and shows Karlee a picture from his wedding day. I'd normally think that was cheesy, but these days, I find myself liking the cheesy stuff.

"And you have a daughter, Elli, am I right?" she asks Daniel.

"Yes, but I don't have a picture in my wallet like this guy." Daniel laughs and playfully punches Brant's arm.

"No, but he's got a ton of pictures of her in magnetic picture frames all over his toolbox," I say, giving him a pointed look. "Don't act like you're not just as proud of Elli as Brant is of Liam."

Daniel laughs. "You're right." He goes to his toolbox and grabs a frame from the box. "Here she is." He shows Karlee the picture.

"They're cute kids." She hands him back the frame.

"You'll have to meet them sometime," Brant says, shooting me a meaningful look. "I'm sure Morgan and Reese would love to get to know you, too."

"All in good time," I say, shaking my head. "We just started dating. Don't scare her off yet."

Daniel laughs. "It was nice to meet you, Karlee. I hope we see you again soon."

Brant says something similar, and Karlee responds politely.

After saying goodbye to the guys, Karlee says she needs to go get ready for work.

"I'll walk you to your car," I say, setting the cookie container on my toolbox.

"Thanks for introducing me to them. They seem like great friends."

"They are," I say, smiling. "Usually. I'm sorry if they were overwhelming."

She stops at her car and turns to me. "They were great, really. I'd love to meet Morgan and Reese sometime."

"In that case, how would you feel about having dinner with everyone Sunday afternoon? You're off right?" I ask.

"I am. Are you sure you're ready for that?" she asks.

"Why not? Are you already planning on breaking up with me?"

She blushes. "No, but—well, we haven't exactly defined this." She waves her finger between us. "I mean. Are we exclusively dating, or open to dating other people, or..."

I step closer to her. "Karlee," she stops talking and looks up at me. "I'd like to be exclusive if that works for you."

She nods. "I don't date more than one person anyway, so that works for me."

My hand cups her cheek. "I'd like to kiss you. Is that okay?"

She closes her eyes and takes a deep breath. "Yes," she says in a breathy whisper.

Leaning closer, I brush my lips across hers. The electricity bouncing between us takes me by surprise. Her soft lips press into mine, and I feel like I'm vibrating.

After a few moments, we part. Her eyes are glassy, and her cheeks pink. It's my new favorite look on her.

"That was . . ." She stops, searching for the right word. "Amazing."

I drop my forehead to hers. "You're amazing, Karlee. Now you should go get ready for work or I'll keep you here kissing you goodbye all day. I'll see you tomorrow?"

She nods. "Tomorrow."

I open her car door, and she slides inside. "Drive safe." I close her door and step back, watching her pull out of the driveway with my heart in the palm of her hand.

Daniel is leaning against my toolbox, a chocolate chip cookie in his hand, when I finally make it back inside.

"What took you so long?" he asks, biting into the cookie and groaning. "These are so good. You should try one," he says, handing me the container.

"Yeah, that was supposed to be for me." I chuckle and take a cookie before putting the container back on the toolbox. "I was helping Karlee to her car."

He laughs, bits of cookie flying out of his mouth. "Is that what the kids are calling it these days?"

I swallow my bite of cookie and frown. "What are you talking about?"

"Come on, Evan. I saw you give her a goodbye kiss. You must really like her for you to introduce her to us and kiss her in public." Daniel sits down on the rolling stool I have in my bay and crosses his legs. "Spill it."

"Wait!" Brant calls, running from the office. "Wait for me. I had a call." He rushes into my bay, holding a folding chair. He flips it open and sits down. "Pass me one of those," he says, pointing to Daniel's cookie. "Then I'll be ready."

Daniel passes Brant a cookie, and they both look at me expectantly.

I hold up my hands in defense. "I don't know what this is—some kind of intervention or something?"

They laugh.

"I'm serious, guys," I say, taking the cookie container and locking it in a drawer. "What's going on?"

"You tell us," Brant says, happily munching on the cookie. "You've always said you're not settling down. After Louise, we both thought you were done with women. I know that hurt."

"Wait." I hold up my hand to stop him. "You knew about Louise?"

Daniel and Brant share a look.

"Evan, it made the papers," Daniel says matter-of-factly.

"You two had been dating a long time, so naturally people talked," Brant said.

"Great." I grab a wrench and duck under the hood of the car I was working on. I knew there'd been gossip, but I'd hoped it hadn't made its way through everyone in Piney Brook.

"No one blames you, Evan," Daniel says. "She made her own choices that night."

"We're just thrilled to see you opening up again, Evan. I know how important family is to you." Brant frowns. "I didn't mean to open an old wound, but you need to know that wasn't on you. You didn't fail her."

I sigh. "Logically, I know you're right, but it still stings."

"So, tell us about Karlee," Daniel says, trying to lighten the mood.

I smile. "She's great. She is funny, caring, and easy to talk to ..."

"By the kiss in the parking lot, and how happy you've been this week, am I to assume you've already been on a date?" Brant smiles encouragingly.

"Yeah, I took her to the lookout. We had a picnic, watched the sunset, and danced under the stars. It was the best date I've ever had."

Daniel stands and slaps my shoulder. "My guy! I think I'm going to steal that idea."

I laugh. "Go ahead, I'm sure it's been done a million times." I sway a bit, remembering how she felt in my arms. "She's honestly the most laid-back woman I've ever met. We have a lot in common, including not really being into the bar scene like most people our age."

Daniel and Brant nod. "I'm sure that's important after all you've been through."

"It is."

"So, will she be at dinner Sunday?" Daniel asks, crossing his fingers and holding them in the air.

"Yeah, I asked her before she left. She said she'd come."

Brant stands and folds the chair back up. "Well, that means I need to tell Morgan to plan for one more." He turns to walk away, rubbing his hands together delightedly. "I'm happy for you, Evan. You deserve this."

I don't know what to say to that, so I just nod my head in acceptance.

"So," Daniel says mischievously. "It appears I'm not the only one who is—what did you call it? Love drunk?"

I shake my head at his antics. "No one said anything about the L word."

"No," he says in agreement. "But you did once say you won't bring anyone around unless it's serious." He raises his eyebrows. "Are you saying this isn't serious?"

I blush. "I don't know what it is. Somewhere in the middle?"

He laughs. "Okay, whatever you say. By the way, I'm taking off early today. Elli is with Heather, and Reese is finishing up early today. I guess she and Morgan got the classroom all set up in record time."

I nod and toss him a rag. "Don't forget to clean up before you see her. She might not like the smell of grease." I pinch my nose as if he stinks, and laugh.

"Get back to work," he says, snapping a shop towel at me. "See you Sunday."

"Are you sure it's okay that I'm here," Karlee asks as we get out of the truck at Brant's house Sunday afternoon.

"Of course," I say, kissing her nose. "Besides, I want you to meet Morgan and Reese, and the kids."

She nods. "Okay."

I reach into the bed of the truck and pull out the box of things I brought for Elli and Liam. Some bubbles, play dough, and a game they can play outside.

"Do you always bring things for the kids?" Karlee asks.

"No, but they love it when I do," I say, and grin.

We walk into the house, and the talking stops. "Well, hello there. Don't stop on our account," I say, shaking my head. Could they be anymore obvious?

Morgan steps forward and draws Karlee into a hug. "You must be Karlee. We've heard so much about you."

"You have?" Karlee and I ask at the same time.

Morgan laughs. "Brant and Daniel have been telling us for weeks about this new neighbor that had Evan tied up in knots. I can see why. You're absolutely gorgeous."

"Thank you," Karlee says, leaning into my side.

"Hi, I'm Reese." Thankfully, she gives Karlee a bit more space.

"Nice to meet you both."

Just then, the back door slides open with a bang and Elli and Liam come rushing in. "Uncle Evan! Where's your new girlfriend?" Elli calls from the kitchen.

Everyone snickers, and Karlee blushes.

"We're in here Elli," Reese calls.

Elli and Liam skid to a stop in front of Karlee. "Hello," Elli says quietly.

"Karlee, this is Elli," I say, reaching out and ruffling her hair. "And this handsome gentleman is Liam."

Liam waves from his spot behind Elli.

"Nice to meet you," Karlee says, dropping to their level. "I hear you have your Uncle Evan wrapped around your finger." She winks at the kids.

"Yeah," Liam says. "He's the funnest."

"Hey," Brant calls from his spot near the stove.

"Sorry, Daddy," Liam says before grabbing Elli's hand and dragging her back outside.

"So, those were the kids," Morgan says, laughing. "Why don't you come sit down with us on the porch? The guys are cooking tonight."

Karlee looks at me, and I shrug.

"That sounds great."

The girls step out the sliding glass door, and I lean against the counter watching Karlee settle into an adirondack chair.

"You really have it bad," Daniel says, passing me a bottle of water.

"But, to be fair, we all do," Brant says. He hands me a knife and points to the counter where the ingredients for a salad are all laid out. "Mind making the salad?"

I get started chopping vegetables and throwing them in the bowl. Laughter drifts through the open window, and I sneak a peek at the three women relaxing outside.

"They seem to be getting along," Daniel says, adding sauce to the browned meat.

"I'm glad. Karlee doesn't know a lot of people here yet." I glance out the window and catch her with her head tilted back, the sun shining on her face, and smile. "She could use some good friends, I think."

A few minutes later, Brant has dinner on the table, and a smaller foldout table set up for Liam and Elli. Daniel goes outside and calls everyone in while I pull the garlic bread from the oven.

"What are we having?" Liam asks, plopping into his seat at the smaller table.

"Spaghetti," Brant says, putting two plates on the table for the kids.

I add a piece of garlic bread to each plate before setting the tray on the adult table.

Karlee stands off to the side, while everyone else takes a seat. I pull out the chair next to me. "You can sit here, sunshine."

Chapter Seventeen

Karlee

"Aww," Morgan says, batting her eyelashes. "You have a cute nickname for her."

I am certain my face matches the spaghetti sauce as I sit down in the seat next to Evan. He reaches over and gives my knee a little squeeze.

"Don't embarrass her, babe," Brant says, handing her an extra piece of garlic bread.

"Sorry!" she says quickly. "I was teasing Evan. I didn't mean to embarrass you. Besides, I think it's sweet."

Evan grins and leans over to kiss my red cheek. "I love it when you blush," he says quietly so only I can hear him.

"So, Uncle Evan," Elli says, pushing her spaghetti around on her plate. "Is Ms. Karlee going to be your new wife?"

I freeze mid bite. This is awkward. "We just started dating, Elli girl, give us some time. It might happen." He reaches for my hand and rubs his thumb across my fingers before going back to eating.

"But Daddy and Reese are..." she starts.

"Also dating," Daniel says quickly, giving her a pointed look.

Her eyes go wide, and she nods her head before looking down at her plate again. "Yeah," she mumbles at the plate.

"Well," Brant says, looking at Morgan. "We have something to share."

Everyone stops eating. It's as if the whole room is holding its breath. I don't even know them well, and I'm on pins and needles.

"Well!" Reese exclaims after a long pause.

"We're expecting," Morgan says, touching Brant's shoulder.

Daniel and Evan both get up and slap Brant on the back, offering him their congratulations.

Reese jumps up from her seat and gives Morgan a huge hug. "I knew it!"

Morgan laughs. "There's no way you knew. We just found out yesterday."

"I did too. You can just tell, right, Karlee?"

I'm like a deer in headlights.

"No one just knows," Evan says, coming to my rescue. "That's why they sell those little tests."

"When are you due?" Reese asks, opening up the calendar app on her phone.

Morgan laughs. "Sometime in late April or early May, I think."

Reese sighs. "An anniversary baby," she says, looking between the two of them. "How sweet."

Brant is beaming. "I can't wait to add to our family."

Liam runs over to Morgan and whispers something in her ear. She nods her head and he claps his hands before running back to the little table. He doesn't even make it into his seat before he starts talking. "I'm going to be a big brother!" he yells.

Elli grins. "I hope you have a sister."

Liam's face falls. "No," he says, shaking his head. "I'm having a baby brother."

Brant laughs and calls Liam over. "It doesn't work like that," he says, trying to find a way to explain it to Liam. "You don't get to choose."

Liam nods his head. "Yes you do. I've been wishing for a baby brother since you got married, and we all know my wishes come true."

He looks around the table and squints his eyes at Evan. "Well, most of them."

Evan laughs. "What's that supposed to mean?"

"Nothing," Elli shouts, giving Liam a cross look.

We all laugh. These two are something else.

After dinner, the men clean up, insisting that we rest. It's strange. Growing up in a single-parent household, we always did the cooking and the cleaning. My grandpa never pitched in. Those were "women's chores" he'd say.

"Do they always cook and clean?" I ask Morgan and Reese.

"Not always. We rotate houses when we get together, and we try to rotate who's responsible for the meals. That way, it's not too much for anyone." Morgan leans back in the reclining chair in the living room.

"You'll see," Reese says confidently.

"Oh, I don't know." I glance to the kitchen where Evan and Daniel are engaged in a dish-bubble brawl. "I don't think we're there yet. We just started dating. Besides, our apartments are not that big."

Morgan frowns. "You mean *you're* not there yet. Because from where I sit, he seems all in."

I look at her for a minute. "He can't be all in yet, we haven't been together very long." Can he? I have to admit, he's made his way past my defenses. Maybe . . .

Laughter rings out from the kitchen area, and I glance over to see Evan with bubbles in his hair. He's laughing and relaxed, enjoying the back-and-forth with his friends. He glances at me and winks. My stomach flip-flops and I realize I'm in deep. I think I'm falling for my next-door neighbor.

Reese shakes her head and points to the kitchen. "That man is all in." She pauses. "Do you know he's never brought a girl around Brant and Daniel?"

I shake my head. "I'm sure that's not true." Evan said he didn't date much, but surely he's brought some women around.

Morgan nods. "It is. He said he'd never bring anyone around that he wasn't sure would be here for the long haul. If that's not all in, I don't know what is."

I look at Evan again. Could he really be so sure this soon?

"Karlee," Reese says, pulling my attention back to the conversation. "Don't hurt him. He's one of the good ones. These guys, once they love you… they love hard."

I nod. I hadn't considered it might be me who hurts someone.

A few hours later—after playing a loud game of rummy while the kids played outside—we are in the car heading back home. "What did you think?" Evan asks. "Too much?"

Elli and Liam had continued to make awkward comments throughout the night. They kept giving each other sly looks every few minutes. But they're cute kids. Apparently since Morgan and Brant got married, they've made it their mission to make sure all the guys find their "happily ever after." It's sweet, even if it is a bit misguided.

"It was great. Morgan and Reese are wonderful. We exchanged numbers. I hope that's okay." I don't want Evan to feel like I'm encroaching on his friend group. If things go south, I don't want to cause ripples. I know how hard it was to lose a significant other and a best friend at the same time. I wouldn't wish that on anyone.

"That's great. I'm glad you got along." Evan's grin is the biggest I've ever seen on him. "I want you to have friends, Karlee. Morgan and Reese, well, they're some of the best friends you could have. They're like family to me."

I nod, unsure what it would be like to have a group of friends who regularly got together and enjoyed each other's company. It was nice to be a part of.

Evan walks me to my door when we get back to the apartments and says, "Thanks for coming with me tonight. It means a lot that you enjoyed hanging out with my friends."

I nod. "It was fun. Thanks for inviting me."

"When can I see you again?" he asks, placing his hands on the door frame boxing me in.

"I work the next few nights," I say, trying not to breathe him in. His scent is intoxicating.

"Then I should give you a few goodnight kisses to hold us both over. What do you think?"

"It's worth a shot," I say, leaning forward, then pressing my lips to his.

Monday evening, I find myself pulling into the parking lot of the Coffee Loft for a pre-shift pick-me-up. The little shop is located in the old brick strip mall that makes up the part of Main Street near the hospital, making it the perfect spot to grab a coffee before work. Its old red bricks, faded in the sun, give the little shop character.

Stepping inside, I inhale the aroma of freshly ground coffee beans and sigh.

"Hey there, girlfriend," the barista with the blue hair calls. "It's been a while."

I shake my head. "Hi. Lacey, right?"

"Yep, what can I get you?"

I look at the menu, trying to decide if I want hot or cold. "How about the largest pumpkin cream cold brew you can make?"

Lacey smiles. "Rough day?"

"I'm just tired," I say, covering my mouth as I yawn again.

"Is that handsome boyfriend keeping you out too late?" She grins. "If you ever decide to ditch him, I'll take him off your hands."

I laugh. "I think I'll hold on to him for a bit, but I'll keep that in mind."

Lacey nods and gets started making my drink. A few minutes later, she holds up a large cup. "Your pumpkin cream iced brew."

"Thanks," I say, taking the large iced coffee. "I am surprised you have pumpkin flavors this early."

"Pumpkin seems to be a favorite starting at the beginning of August. It doesn't matter how hot it is—people are just ready for fall."

I grin. "Makes sense." I hold up the cup. "As you can see, I like pumpkin almost year round. Have a good night, Lacey."

"Thanks. You too."

Fifteen minutes later, I'm walking off the elevator onto the fourth floor. There's yelling coming from down the hall, so I sprint off the elevator and drop my stuff in the nurse's station without stopping. Running down the hall, I stop at the room with all the commotion.

"What's happening?" I ask as I step into the room.

Mona looks at me over the head of the phlebotomist and raises an eyebrow. "We have a patient who doesn't like to have blood drawn."

Taking deep breaths, I will my heart rate to calm. "I see," I pant. Still out of breath from running. "Have you tried numbing cream?"

Mona looks at the phlebotomist.

"No, it's just a quick draw. We don't generally use numbing cream on adult patients."

I roll my eyes and walk closer to the bed. "Hi, I'm Karlee. I'm one of the nurses who will be working tonight. I take it you don't like having your blood drawn?"

The young woman in the bed looks like she can't be older than nineteen. "No." She whimpers as the needle comes into sight again.

"Okay, I understand. It can be scary." I try to soothe her with my voice. "How about we apply some numbing cream so you won't feel that pinch when it goes in? Can we give that a try?"

The young woman looks at me, her eyes wide and frantic. "Does that actually help?"

"Yes," I say.

"No," the phlebotomist says at the same time.

I shoot her an evil look. I've never worked with this one before, but patient care requires a softer touch than this. She should know better.

"It does, it just takes a few minutes to work," I assure her.

"Can I speak to you in the hall?" the phlebotomist says, and stomps out ahead of me.

"Yes?"

"I don't have time to coddle the adult patients. I've got other people on my list that I still need to get to."

"Listen—" I lean down to see her name on her name tag. "Listen, Julie. This 'adult' is no more than nineteen years old and scared out of her mind. Rub the cream on and come back in thirty minutes. That should be plenty of time for you to do another patient or two."

She sighs. "Fine."

"Thank you," I say sweetly, turning on my heel and re-entering the room. "Julie here is going to apply the numbing cream. It takes some time to work fully, so she will come back in thirty minutes. In the meantime, can I get you some water or juice?"

Nights like last night are hard. Sadly, the run-in with Cranky Julie, as I'm now calling her, was the easiest part of my night.

Around four a.m., we had a code blue, but were unable to save the patient. I hate when we lose someone. It's part of why I don't work in the emergency room. It takes a huge emotional toll on me. The linen closet in the hall and I became good friends last night.

When I finally got to my car after my shift, I climbed in and just sat there for a minute letting the feelings of the night wash over me. I cried. Again. The gentleman had been young. In his early forties. He had a family—a wife and two kids—who don't get to hug him anymore, feel his love.

Evan's smile flashes before my eyes, and I can't help but feel like I'm already half in love with this man. I couldn't imagine losing him from my life.

Wiping my eyes, I start the car and make my way home. A hot shower and some sleep should help me regroup.

Pulling into the parking space in front of my building, I question whether or not I could just sleep in my car. Exhaustion weighs on me, making my limbs feel heavy. Sighing, I open my door and step out. I need my bed.

I finally make it to the top of the stairs and unlock the door, but then I hear Evan's door open behind me. I could really use the comfort of his hug right about now. Turning around, I step forward and find myself staring at a woman's back coming out of Evan's apartment. Insecurities slam into me as I recall feeling sideswiped when Patrick told me he'd moved on with someone else.

"My lips are still tingling from your kisses this morning," she says into her phone. She giggles and says something else I don't quite catch over the blood rushing through my ears.

She hangs up the phone and starts to turn around, but I quickly slip inside my apartment and lock the door. Tears come hot and heavy, making my crying session from earlier seem nonexistent.

No. This cannot be happening to me again.

Chapter Eighteen

Evan

I'M JUST CLIMBING INTO bed when I hear my phone ringing in the other room. Groaning, I get up and rush to grab it. Tracey's number flashes across the screen, so I swipe to answer.

"Hey, sis, what's up?"

"You sound happy," Tracey says instead of a greeting. "Did you have a nice time on your date?"

I laugh. Of course she'd ask. "Yep." No sense denying it.

"Good for you," Tracey says, sounding genuinely happy for me. "Details?"

"Not tonight," I say, smiling at her enthusiasm. "It's late, and I have to work in the morning."

"All right, fine." She huffs playfully. "Listen, I hate to ask, but can I use your washer and dryer in the morning? Ours is on the fritz, and we need clean clothes."

"Sure, help yourself." I head to the washer and dryer to make sure they're empty for her.

"Can I pop over and say hi to Karlee?"

I chuckle. "Can't wait, huh?"

"No, I'm too excited." She laughs. "I promise I'll be good. I won't even tell her any embarrassing stories about you."

"Thanks, sis. She works nights, and sleeps during the day. If you see her in the hall, you can introduce yourself, but don't wake her up, okay?"

"Fine," Tracey says, sighing. "I won't wake her up. Thanks for letting me use your stuff."

"No problem," I say, meaning it. That's what family's for. "I'll see you in the morning."

We end the call, and I fall into bed, my mind already on Karlee, and how she's doing at work. I can't remember a time I felt so content. Karlee fit right in with my friends, and I know my family will love her. Our date went even better than I expected. I wonder what we can do for our second date.

"What are you smiling about over there?" Daniel calls from across the shop. "Care to share with the class?"

I laugh. "Sure, I'll share with you as soon as you tell me what Elli was really going to say the other night at dinner." I give him a knowing look.

"Oh, shoot. May as well get Brant."

I grin. This is going to be good.

A few minutes later, we are all in Daniel's bay, waiting for him to gather his thoughts.

"So, as Evan mentioned, Elli almost let something big slip at dinner Sunday." He walks to his toolbox, unlocks the top drawer and digs something out. He comes to stand in front of us and pops open the lid to the small box.

"Congratulations!" Brant and I say at the same time.

"When are you popping the question?"

"I'm planning to rent the lake house again for Labor Day. I want to invite our families to stay with us for the weekend, but I'd love it if you guys could make it up on Saturday and surprise her when I pop the question."

I hesitate. I'd been hoping to set the routine of having an early dinner with Karlee before her shift on the weekends.

"It would mean a lot to her if we had our framily there." He grins.

"Framily?" Brant asks. "What the heck is that?"

"Friends who are family. Elli made it up, and I thought it fit." Daniel shrugs. "Can you make it?"

"Of course," I say, patting him on the shoulder. "I don't know if Karlee can make it with work, but I'll be there."

"We'll be there too," Brant says. "I'll have to figure out a way to keep Morgan from giving it away, though. Maybe I'll tell her I'm planning a surprise getaway for us that weekend." He laughs. "She'll be too excited to keep this secret for very long."

"Thanks, Brant." Daniel puts the ring box back in the drawer and locks it.

"I guess that just leaves you," Brant says, pointing a finger in my direction.

"Leaves me what?" I ask, holding my hands in front of my body in defense.

Daniel laughs. "You're the only one not engaged. Yet."

I shake my head. "Too soon," I say, laughing. "Karlee and I aren't old like you two. We have time."

Brant throws a rag in my direction and Daniel scoffs.

"Get back to work, kid."

I head back over to my bay and finish draining the oil from the older sedan. Twenty-six is still young, right? There's no rush to get married. Though, now that they've put it out there, I can't help imagining my ring on Karlee's finger. I wonder if she'd want something unique, or the standard princess cut diamond engagement ring?

I've just finished putting oil into the car I'm working on when my phone rings. Wiping my hands on a clean cloth, I grab the phone and hit answer when I see my sister's name on the caller ID.

"Hey, Tracey. Did you get your laundry done?"

"I did. Where do you want me to leave your key?"

"Just hold on to it. I'll get it when I see you next time," I say. "Did you meet Karlee?"

Tracey sighs. "No, I guess I'll have to wait."

I laugh. "I'm sure it won't be too long."

"All right," she says. "I hope not."

"Listen, I've got to go. I need to get back to work." Though, now I'm imagining Karlee at my parents' house, laughing and playing with Brody and Emilia. I smile. I can't wait for her to meet my family.

Tracey and I say our goodbyes and hang up after I promise to ask Karlee to the next family dinner.

By the time I get home that afternoon, Karlee's car is already gone. Disappointment sits heavy on my chest. I'd hoped to spend a few minutes with her before she went to work. I decide to send her a text.

Evan: Hey, sunshine, I hope you have a great night at work. I'm sorry I missed you this evening. I can't wait to see you again.

Maybe I'll take her some flowers at work after dinner. Women like that, right?

When I walk up the stairs, I'm surprised to find Heath sitting on my doorstep. "Hey man, what are you doing here?"

Heath looks up at me sadly. "I was hoping you were free tonight." He stands and leans against the wall while I open the door.

"I am," I say, stepping inside and taking off my work boots. "You okay?"

Heath shrugs. "It's been a long day. Do you mind if I just hang out here for a while? I need to get out of the house."

"No problem. Want a Coke or a glass of water?" I reach in the fridge and grab myself a Coke.

"Coke's fine. Thanks."

I grab him a can of Coke as well and head to the living room. Handing him a can, I set mine down on the coffee table and gesture to my clothes. "I'm going to change out of these. I'll be right back."

He nods, and cracks open his can. "All right."

It looks like taking Karlee flowers is off the table. I grab my phone and check for any missed messages. I feel like a schoolboy with his first crush as much as I check my phone hoping to hear from her.

I shake my head and pull on a pair of basketball shorts and a t-shirt.

"Okay, that's better," I say, walking back into the living room. I sit down on the couch and open my drink. "So, what's up?"

Heath looks everywhere but at me. "I tried to talk to her today."

"Who?" I ask, but I suspect I already know.

"Gabby."

"Why today?" I ask, wondering why, after avoiding her for the past few months, he'd decided to try again. I take a sip of my drink, giving him some time to gather his thoughts.

"I don't know, man. All this stuff with Mom... It makes me realize life's short, you know."

I nod my head. "I can see that."

"She didn't want to talk to me. I really messed up." He looks at me. "How do I fix it?"

I bark out a laugh. "Dude, I have no idea. Until recently, I had no interest in relationships, remember?"

Heath sits back, pressing deep into the cushions. "Relationships are hard."

"Relationships are work," I say. "But if you're with the right person, are they still hard?"

Heath looks at me for a long moment. "The right person, huh?"

I hesitate. I know something happened between him and Gabby, and he's obviously hurting, but he's also my friend. "Yeah, I think she might be."

He nods. "Happiness looks good on you."

"So," I say, trying to change the subject. "What are you going to do now?"

Heath takes a drink of his Coke before answering. "I'm not sure."

"Do you think she's your person?" I ask.

"Maybe," Heath says. "I thought she was, but now she won't even talk to me."

We sit quietly for a minute, both lost in thought before Heath stands. "I'm going to go," he says. "Mom has an early appointment, and I need some rest."

I walk him to the door and lock it behind him when he leaves, thoughts of Karlee running on a loop through my mind. It may be too soon, but I'm falling for her anyway.

I'm up before my alarm goes off. I missed Karlee last night, but I'm hoping to catch her when she gets home this morning. I dreamt of her soft kisses and sweet smile last night. Yeah, I've got it bad.

I'm pacing near the front door, waiting to hear her come up the steps. Mittens eyes me from his spot on the couch, hissing every time I walk by. Sorry, kitty, I'm too excited to sit down. I glance at the clock. Seven forty-five. She should have been home ages ago. Opening the blinds, I take a look in the parking lot. Her car is there. How did I miss her coming home?

I glance at the time on my phone. I have to leave or I'll be late, and I have a big job coming in today. Rushing back to my apartment, I find a pen and a sticky note. Scribbling a message, I grab my keys and head out. I stick the note to her door and hope it doesn't fly away. I'm feeling like she's avoiding me, but that can't be right.

I start the truck and turn on the radio. It's still set to Karlee's favorite station. The first song we danced to up at the lookout is playing, making my heart skip a beat. I rub my hand over my heart. Thoughts of dancing with her at our wedding one day send a warm fuzzy feeling through my chest. I never thought I'd want to get married after things ended so badly with Louise, but Karlee makes me want it all.

Chapter Nineteen

Karlee

"You're in early again," Mona says when I walk onto the floor Wednesday.

"Yep," I say, refusing to give her any more information. I don't even know what I'd say. *Oh, yeah. Evan is cheating on me, and now I have to live across from him until my lease is up, or until he leaves to start a new life with her.* Nope, I don't think that would go over well. I shudder to think how quickly that gossip would make its way around town. No thanks.

"Okay," she says, rolling the med cart into a room. "I'm here if you want to talk."

I go sit behind the nurse's station and lay my head on my arms. I've not slept well since my shift Monday when we lost the patient. I'd thought that shift was terrible... then I came home to see a woman leaving Evan's apartment. I've been avoiding him. He's sent me several texts wanting to talk, but I just can't. Not yet. I'm not strong enough yet. I need more time to detach. How is he buried so deep already?

I was less hurt when I found out Patrick had cheated on me with my best friend, for Pete's sake. Then I was mostly mad that my dreams were going up in flames and there was nothing I could do about it. Losing Patrick was an afterthought. The idea of losing Evan makes my heart feel like it's cracked in two.

"Karlee, I'm so glad you're here. They are short staffed in the ER and could use some help."

I lift my head off my arms. "Can someone else do it? I'm not in a good space to work in the ER."

Amanda looks at me pointedly. "This floor has three on tonight, and we can manage with two, but neither of the other two have any emergency experience. It's you, Karlee."

I sigh and gather my things. "Okay," I say gruffly. "See you later."

I make my way down to the ER. The very last place I'd like to be right now. Looking around, I spot the charge nurse and head in his direction. "Hey, Amanda sent me down here to cover."

"Great," he says, relief evident in his voice. "If you could work up room one right now, that would be amazing."

I nod and head in that direction. Setting my stuff behind the nurse's station out of the way, I grab the tablet and head into room one. I knock softly before opening the door, reading the tablet as I step inside. A few minutes later, I'm back at the nurse's station when I see her. The woman I saw sneaking out of Evan's apartment. She's walking in with a little boy who looks miserable. *You have got to be kidding me.*

I duck my head and try not to be noticed.

The charge nurse stops and leans his hip on the counter. "Six-year-old boy, possible concussion," he says, nodding his head in the direction of the room they went into. "I've got it for now, but I may need you to take over. I might be getting called into surgery in a few minutes."

I'm beginning to think if it weren't for bad luck, I'd have no luck at all. I don't have time to respond before he walks away. Let's just hope that doesn't happen.

I look over the orders that came in for my patient and stand. I grab the antibiotics the doctor ordered and head to the room. Maybe this patient will keep me busy enough I won't have time to take over.

Stepping back into the hallway, I bump into someone.

"Hello, I don't think I've seen you in the emergency room before," a deep voice says from beside me. "I'm Dr. Sullivan."

Finally, I get to meet the doctor who has captured more than one nurse's attention at Piney Brook General. "Karlee," I say, holding out my name tag. "I'm filling in for the night."

He nods. His dark, almost black, hair is cropped close on the sides and a bit longer on the top. Eyes the color of moss have little wrinkle lines beside them. He looks tired. Dr. Sullivan is handsome, and I can see why he's captured the female attention. But there's no spark. He doesn't make me feel warm and tingly, like Evan does.

Tears burn the back of my eyes, and I blink rapidly to hold them off. I'm at work. I will not cry over a man at work. No matter how I might feel about him.

"I'm glad for the help. We have a nurse out with the flu tonight."

"Happy to help," I say, even though I'd rather be anywhere than here.

He points to room three. "What's happening?"

I shrug. "Not sure," I say, hoping I don't sound rattled. "Derick was working that room up, but I think it was a little boy with a possible concussion."

Dr. Sullivan nods. "I think he's busy right now. Care to assist?"

"Uh, sure," I stammer.

"Let's go in and check it out."

He opens the door wide and steps inside, holding it open for me to slip through as well. Surprise makes my eyebrows shoot up when I notice the woman standing with a very handsome man, who is very clearly not Evan. He's got his arm around her and she's leaning into him for support. His blond curly hair matches the young boy's, and I'd bet money he's the father.

I shake my head and get focused on my job. It doesn't matter that Evan had a strange woman in his apartment early in the morning, that she has a child, or that she's cuddled up with some other man. I have to be professional.

"I'm Dr. Sullivan," the doctor says, introducing himself. Thankfully, he jumps right in asking questions and evaluating the little boy.

"So, what happened?" Dr. Sullivan asks the woman, pushing up his sleeves and washing his hands.

"He was jumping around pretending he was Spiderman and went over the back of the chair in the living room. Landed right on his head."

"Ouch, that sounds like it hurt, Spidey."

The little boy nods.

"Any vomiting, dizziness?" Dr. Sullivan asks.

"He threw up right after it happened, which is why I brought him in. He's done crazier things than this, but he's never thrown up." She sounds worried, and I can't help but feel for her. I can't imagine how it must feel when your child hurts themselves.

I stand quietly in the corner entering the information into the system, thankful that she doesn't recognize me.

"What's your name, little guy?"

The young boy looks at his mother and she nods. "Brody," he says, sniffling.

"Nice to meet you, Brody. My name is Dr. Sully." He grabs a glove from the box on the counter and blows it up, tying it off at the bottom creating a weird hand balloon. "What happened tonight?" He hands the boy the balloon and starts his exam.

"I was being Spidey, and I falled of the chair and hit my head. I don't feel so good." He wiggles back into his mom, who is holding him tight.

She seems like a great mother. Ugh. I don't want to find things I like about her. Not when she's the reason my relationship with Evan is over already.

He said he wants to be exclusive, and then I find another woman leaving his apartment in the morning. I didn't think he'd do something like that, but the proof is in the pudding. Or the landing, as it were.

"Uh, oh. You have to be super careful when you're doing superhero work," Dr. Sullivan says, smiling. "All right, Mom, I think he has a mild concussion, but we are going to get a CT scan to rule out anything more serious."

She nods. "Thank you."

"Where's Brody?" A familiar voice rings out in the hallway.

Evan? I quickly look at the man standing at the bedside. He doesn't seem the least bit concerned. I panic, looking around the room for some secret exit or portal that will get me out of this ridiculous situation.

"In here," the woman calls.

I stare at her in shock. Isn't she worried that their paths will cross? They seem too familiar to have been divorced. At least my parents never held each other like that after their divorce, and before Dad just disappeared from our lives.

Evan steps through the door and stops. "Karlee?"

I give him a small wave, unsure what to do. This is bad. Nervous laughter bubbles past my lips and I slap a hand over my mouth to stop it.

"I didn't realize you worked on this floor, too."

"I don't, usually. They were short-staffed tonight. I'm just filling in."

He nods.

Dr. Sullivan reaches out his hand. "Nice to meet you…"

"This is my brother, Evan," the woman says as Evan shakes the doctor's hand.

Brother? Did she say her brother? I look at Evan who is now sitting next to Brody on the bed. Oh boy.

"Are you still feeling like you might throw up?" Dr. Sullivan asks Brody, cutting through my fog.

Brody nods his head and closes his eyes.

"Your head still hurting?" he asks.

Brody nods again, keeping his eyes shut, and his head pressed against his mother for comfort.

"All right, Ms. Karlee will get you something to help your tummy and the ouchies too, okay?"

Brody mumbles something I'm guessing is "okay," and turns, wrapping his arms around his mom.

"We'll be back soon," Dr. Sullivan says, motioning for me to leave the room first.

"Go ahead and order scans. I think he will be okay, but I'd rather rule out anything serious before we let him go home. I'll put in a prescription for the nausea medicine and some Motrin." He types something into the computer. "Page me if anything happens, or when we get results."

"Will do." I take a deep breath, and then another. I've got some apologizing to do.

I slide into an empty linen closet and take a deep breath. What is my life coming to? I feel awful for jumping to conclusions. And for essentially ghosting Evan. I should have talked to him, not assumed he was just like Patrick. I'd thought I'd lost him, but I hadn't.

After a few minutes of deep breathing, the phone rings in the nurses' station reminding me I can't stay inside this closet forever. I smooth down my scrubs, refasten my hair in a bun, and head back onto the floor. I finish checking on the other rooms I've been assigned while I wait for the orders to go through. Grabbing the nausea medicine and Motrin, I head back into room three.

"Here we are," I say, opening the door. I make my way to where Brody is now running a toy car back and forth on the bed in front of him.

"Hey, little guy, I've got some medicine for you." He nods and reaches out his little hand for the medicine cup. "The doctor is giving him some Motrin and some medicine for the upset stomach."

The woman nods.

I hand Brody the little cup and he tips it up and drinks it like a pro. "Thanks," he says, handing it back. Evan pats his leg and smiles at me.

"I'd like to introduce myself," Evan's sister says, stepping forward. "I'm Tracey. I've heard so much about you."

I glance at Evan who is watching this interaction with a huge smile on his face.

"I've heard a lot about you, too."

Tracey pulls me in for a hug. "I'm so glad I finally got to meet you. Though I wish it was under other circumstances. I wanted to introduce myself the other day when I was borrowing Evan's washer and dryer, but I never saw you," she says.

"I..." I start and stop. "That would have been nice," I say.

"This is my husband, Lawrence," she says, pointing to the guy who looks like an older carbon copy of Brody.

"Nice to meet you," he says, and nods.

"You too," I say. "I'll go check on the CT results." I smile at everyone and step into the hallway.

I page Dr. Sullivan and let him know Brody's results are in. A few minutes later, he steps behind the nurses' desk and pulls them up.

"Perfect," he says, making some notes on the computer. "I'll go give them the news, and then you can do the discharge paperwork."

I nod. "Of course."

I take a few minutes to print the papers he noted, and prepare myself before heading into the room.

"You get to go home now," I say, smiling at Brody. "Here is the discharge paperwork." I hand the stack to Tracey. "You don't have to wake him up through the night anymore, but do keep an eye on him. If his symptoms get worse, come back to the ER right away."

She nods. "Thank you, Karlee."

"You're welcome. I noted the time we gave him the Motrin so you'll know when he can have more."

She smiles at me and takes the paperwork.

I hand her a pen and show her where to sign. My eyes are drawn to Evan, who is laughing and playing with Brody.

"Uncle Evan," Brody says sweetly. "Can you get me some ice cream?"

"I think your mom would be mad if I gave you sugar tonight, but how about we have a bros day soon?" Evan ruffles Brody's hair.

Brody grins and nods. "Yeah!"

"Since when have you ever listened to me?" Tracey asks.

"Come on, Tracey. You know I at least try to follow the rules. It's not easy being the favorite uncle when your sister won't let you bribe the kids with cookies and ice cream." Evan winks at me.

"It was nice to meet you, all," I say to Tracey, Lawrence, and Brody. "Y'all have a good night. No more flipping over chairs, Spidey."

I grab for the door, but Evan stops me. "I know you're working, and you're busy, but can we talk when you get home? I feel like you're avoiding me, and I don't like it."

I smile. "We can talk then," I say, stepping out the door. I glance at the clock. I have six hours to figure out how to explain myself. Piece of cake.

CHAPTER TWENTY

Evan

SEEING KARLEE TONIGHT, CONFIRMED the feeling she'd been avoiding me. I don't know whether to be upset or give her some grace. I know she's been through a lot, and that she was hurt when Patrick cheated on her, but I've done nothing to give her the impression I'd do the same. Or at least, I don't think so.

"Thanks for coming," Tracey says, holding Brody close to her chest. "He really scared me this time."

I lean in and give them both a hug. "I'll always be here for you guys."

"She's lovely," Tracey says softly. "I can see why you love her."

"What?" I ask, stunned that my sister has picked up on how I'm feeling.

Tracey grins. "Don't wait too long to let her know how you feel."

Lawrence pulls the minivan to the loading area and opens the door. "Thanks for waiting with them," he says, coming around to help buckle Brody in.

"Where'd you park your car?" I ask Lawrence, looking around.

"I didn't. Your mom dropped me off at the front when I took Emilia to her. That way, we didn't have two cars here."

"Smart." I lean into the car and give Brody a gentle kiss on his forehead. "I love you, little man. Bros day soon, okay?"

Brody nods and settles into the seat.

I watch them pull away and sigh. That kid definitely keeps us all on our toes.

The next morning, I'm sitting outside my apartment door waiting for Karlee to come home. I've already texted Brant to let him know I'll be taking the day off. I've missed her.

When I hear a car door close in the parking lot, my heart quickens. What if she's decided she's not ready to date again, and that's why she's been avoiding me?

I take a deep breath and try to prepare myself for anything.

Karlee reaches the top of the stairs and gives me a sad smile. "Hey."

I stand, unsure if I should go to her or not. I stay put and slide my hands into my pockets. "Hey. Long night?"

She nods. "I don't usually work in the emergency room. It's not my favorite." She motions to her door. "Want to come in?"

I hesitate. She looks tired. "Are you sure? We can talk after you've had a chance to sleep."

She shakes her head and unlocks her door. "I don't want to wait. I owe you an apology."

"Okay," I say, confused. "For what?" I follow her inside her apartment.

"Have a seat, please? I need to go change out of these scrubs."

I nod and make my way toward the couch. Looking around her living room, I can see all the ways she's made it hers. Books are stacked on the coffee table, potted plants are on a little stand near the windows. I smile when I see Peanut sticking her head out of the little hole of her cat house.

"Sorry," Karlee says, coming back into the room and sitting down on the other end of the sofa. "I don't like to sit on the furniture in work clothes."

I nod. "Me either," I say, drinking her in. She looks exhausted. Dark circles take up the space under her eyes, and her lips are pulled down in a soft frown.

"Evan," she says, pausing.

My stomach drops.

"I'm so sorry. I saw Tracey leaving your apartment the other morning and just assumed the worst." Her eyes begin to water and she wipes roughly at the tears. "I should have talked to you about it, but I was scared."

That surprises me. "Scared? Of talking to me?"

She nods. "Well, not of talking to you necessarily, but hearing that you'd picked someone else, too."

My heart aches a bit for the way Patrick treated her. "Karlee, look at me. Please?"

She wipes her eyes again and lifts her gaze to meet mine.

"There's no one else for me to pick. I don't want anyone else."

She nods.

I shake my head and scoot closer to her on the couch. "I don't think you understand," I say, reaching for her hands and holding them in mine. "I am falling in love with you, Karlee. I can see a future with you. Only you."

She sucks in a breath, and tears slide down her face. "You what?"

I smile and wipe the moisture from her cheeks. "You told me once that you wanted to be married, have kids and a home. Do you still want that one day?"

She nods her head.

"Could you see those things with me?" I ask. "Not . . . yet. But one day?"

She closes her eyes, and I feel my future crumbling at her feet.

She squeezes my hands in hers before opening her eyes and nodding her head yes.

Elated, I pull her to me and hold her tight.

"I'm falling for you, Evan. But I'm scared. Part of me wonders when you'll realize that I work too much, or our schedules are too different, and decide that you don't want me anymore."

I lean back, making sure she can see the sincerity in my eyes. "Karlee, that will never happen. Every relationship has things that need to be worked through. We'll figure it out. Besides, you may decide that you want to stay home with our babies one day. Either way, we'll find a way, Karlee."

She gasps. "What did you just say?"

I laugh. "Karlee, I want everything with you. One day, when we're ready. For that to happen, you can't hide from me, or run away every time something happens. You've got to talk me."

She sighs and leans into my shoulder. "I want those things too," she whispers. "I can't promise I'll be great at it, but I promise I'll try to talk things out instead of running from our problems."

"That's all I can ask," I say, running my hands up and down her back. "Actually, I do have one more question," I say.

"What?" she asks.

"Can I kiss you?"

She leans back and looks into my eyes. "I thought you'd never ask."

I gently brush my lips across hers, savoring the softness of her. "I should go so you can get some rest." I say before giving her another soft kiss.

Karlee yawns and nods. "That's a good idea. We're okay?"

"We're more than okay, Sunshine." I give her a quick hug before heading back to my own apartment for a while. "Are you off tonight?" I ask.

She nods, covering another yawn with the back of her hand.

"Can I make you dinner?"

"I'd love that," she says.

I lean in and give her another soft kiss. "See you when you wake up."

It's been a few weeks since Karlee and I shared our feelings, and I've grown more sure about her every day. I can't imagine ever getting tired of that smile of hers.

"You ready, Sunshine?" I call, opening her front door. Today I've planned a big surprise.

She comes out of her room, and I'm breathless. "I'm ready." She pats Peanut on the head and grabs her purse and a light jacket. "Lead the way, handsome." She presses up onto her toes to give me a gentle kiss.

"You look beautiful," I tell her, opening the door for her.

She looks down at the faded jeans and maroon long-sleeved t-shirt she's wearing and laughs. "Yeah, sure I do."

I shake my head. She may not believe me, but she's the most beautiful woman I've ever known.

"Where did you say we were going again?" she asks, locking her door.

"Nice try." I lead her down the stairs and to the truck. "You know it's a surprise."

"Can't blame a girl for trying." She grins and kisses me on the cheek before hopping up into the seat I've come to think of as hers over the last couple of months.

"No, I guess not."

The radio is playing a blend of country and 90s' alternative thanks to a playlist Karlee created. Forty-five minutes later, we pull into a gravel lot splattered with a rainbow of colors and she gasps.

"Paintball? Seriously?" She starts to laugh. "You know I was joking, right?"

"Hey," I say, grinning. "You said paintball was on the table."

The sound of talking and laughter from other players waiting for the eleven a.m. time slot fills the air. Karlee bounces from foot to foot, a huge grin on her face. "I've never done this before," she says excitedly.

"Me either, but I thought it would be a fun date."

"Too bad Morgan and Brant couldn't come," she says, looking around at the other players. "Or Heath—I bet he'd be good at this game."

"Yeah, they frown on pregnant ladies playing. And Heath, well, he avoids anything that reminds him of his time overseas." I'm so glad she's excited about this. When I was setting it up, I wasn't sure she'd go for it.

We get to the registration desk and grab the release forms to sign. After turning those in, we are each given a marker, a mask, and a hopper filled with paintballs. We're shown to a small room where we slide on jumpers to protect our clothes. Just outside, we're given a safety briefing, and an instructor goes over how to use everything before leading us onto the field.

The moment we enter, Karlee's got her game face on. "Let's do this," she says, racing behind a stack of wooden pallets.

Laughing, I follow behind her. "I didn't realize you had such a competitive streak," I say, dipping down beside her. "This is going to be fun."

The sound of paintballs hitting the obstacles starts, and my adrenaline flows. "Ready?" I ask, nodding to a set of barrels close by.

"Yes," Karlee says, getting herself ready.

"On my signal."

Karlee nods, and I peek around the corner. I wave my hand, and we take off, dodging paintballs and running from cover to cover, shooting at anyone we see.

An hour later, we're both covered in colorful paint splatters and laughing. We turn in the gear, and head back to the truck. We weren't the winning team, but I think it's safe to say we both had fun.

"I'm going to be so sore tomorrow," Karlee says, stretching her arms. "But it was worth it. This was an epic date."

"I'm glad you enjoyed it," I say, opening her door.

"It was a lot more fun than I imagined. Though I'm pretty sure I'm going to have a few bruises." She rubs at a spot on her arm that is already turning colors.

"Yeah, I have a few tender spots myself." I start the truck and pull out of the parking lot. "Ready for the next part?"

She laughs and shakes her head. "There's a next part? I thought this was it."

"Nope," I say, flipping on the blinker to head back towards town. "Not even close."

"Are you going to tell me?" She sticks out her bottom lip and makes puppy dog eyes at me.

"Nope," I say again. "But you're welcome to try to guess."

She looks at me for a minute before crossing her arms. "Fine, let me think." She taps her finger on the side of her mouth. "I know! The Fall Festival?"

"I guess you'll have to wait and see."

The Cobb County Fair is the biggest event in the area, and I can't wait to share it with her.

We pull up to the fairgrounds and park. The gang is waiting for us near the front gates, and Karlee squeals when she sees them. "Best date ever," she says, giving me a huge hug.

I buy us tickets and ride tokens, and we all step inside.

"Where to first?" Reese asks, holding Elli's hand. Her shiny new engagement ring sparkling in the sun.

"The bathroom," Morgan says and then laughs. "I forgot how much a woman needs the restroom when she's pregnant."

We offer to wait where we are while the girls make a bathroom trip since neither of the kids needed to go.

"Daddy, can we get funnel cake?" Elli asks Daniel, batting her eyelashes.

"Of course—it's the fair, isn't it?" He pats her on the shoulder. "What do you want to do Liam?"

"I want to ride some rides," Liam says. "And see the cows."

Elli makes a face. "Cows smell."

Brant, Daniel, and I all laugh.

"Don't worry, Elli," Reese says, coming to stand behind her. "The girls will find something else to do when they go to the barn."

Elli lets out a relieved sigh.

Karlee takes my hand and grins. "I'm just excited to be at the fair. I haven't been to one since my grandparents took me when I was little! I have to ride the Ferris wheel today. That was my favorite back then."

"Let's do it," I say, squeezing her hand gently. "I'll take you on it as many times as you want."

"Let's go there first," Liam decides.

We all follow along, making our way through the games and rides to the back where the Ferris wheel is set up.

"Ladies first," I say, letting her step into the car when it's our turn.

We sit patiently as they finish loading everyone on and start the ride.

"This has been a fabulous day," she says, looking around at the colorful view. "I love this time of year. Everything is so beautiful."

My mouth goes dry, and my stomach feels like I swallowed a bucketful of grasshoppers. "It is," I say softly, unable to take my eyes off of her.

She glances at me and smiles, and a soft pink stains her cheeks. "You're sweet."

I tear my eyes away from her finally, and drink in the moment.

When the ride ends, and we step off, we move to a game booth. Ring toss. The kids each try their hand at winning a prize and are disappointed when they only get a cheap plastic duck.

"Let me try," I say, handing the guy a five-dollar bill. Several attempts, and fifty dollars later, I've won each of the kids a stuffed animal.

"This round's on the house." The worker hands me the rings, and I focus. I toss the colorful plastic circle, and it slides right over the top of the golden bottle.

"Wow," the guy says, collecting the rings again. "Hardly anyone hits the grand prize. You can pick from any of the larger items at the top."

I choose a huge stuffed cat with white fur and a tiara. "For you, Sunshine," I say, handing her the gigantic stuffed animal.

She dances in place excitedly. "Thank you," she says, grinning from ear to ear. She hugs me as tight as she can with one arm. "I love it!"

"I love you," I blurt.

Our friends stop talking and stare at me.

"What did you say?" she asks, whipping her head up and meeting my gaze.

"Um." I clear my throat. "I love you."

A smile splits her face, and she laughs. "I love you, too."

Our friends all clap as I take her face in my hands and kiss her softly.

"Ew, Uncle Evan," Liam says loudly, breaking the magic of the moment. "That's gross."

Brant laughs and picks him up, placing him on his shoulder. "You keep thinking that, little buddy."

Karlee leans into my shoulder and laughs.

"Never a dull moment with this group," I say, holding back laughter.

Chapter Twenty-One

Epilogue

Evan

One Year Later

Daniel: They just left the house.

Brant: Great. I'll be waiting outside when you get here.

Daniel: On my way.

I read the texts and swallow hard. Double-checking I have everything, I grab my keys and head out. We all agreed to drive separately, except Brant, who's riding with Daniel on the way there because Morgan has his truck with Reese and Karlee in it. He insisted it was easier to let her drive his truck than to uninstall the car seats. Liam is small, so he still rides in a booster.

Evan: See y'all at the fair.

I hop in the truck and dial Heath's number first.

"Hey, I'm ready," he says in greeting.

I laugh. "I didn't even ask you yet."

"I know, but you've been stressing about the details for days. I'm on my way to pick up the flowers now. It's all a go."

"Thanks, man. I appreciate your help."

Heath laughs. "Like I'd let you do this alone."

I pull into the parking lot fifteen minutes early. I try to take some deep breaths and calm down. Karlee loves me. I love her. Everything will be fine.

I blow out a breath and laugh at myself. Karlee's the love of my life. I can do this. I take a big breath and let it out slowly. Showtime.

I step out of the truck and make my way to the entrance of the Fall Festival. I'm in line waiting to get inside when Brant and Daniel join me.

"This is a great idea," Daniel says, seeing how nervous I am. "I'm sure it's all going to go according to plan."

I laugh. "Nothing in life goes according to plan."

Brant nods his head. "Ain't that the truth."

We make our way inside to the gazebo where a line of kids is waiting to get their faces painted.

"Why did we pick here again?" I ask.

"It's the easiest thing to spot when you get inside," Daniel says, laughing as a kid walks by with paint in his nearly white, blond hair. "Oh man, that's going to stain."

I shoot him a look, and he laughs even harder.

"Oh man, you're a mess."

"Leave him alone," Brant says, patting my back. "Our baby boy is growing up."

"Gee thanks, you're the best friends a guy could hope for."

I spot Heath coming in the gate and looking around. He spots us and heads over.

"These good?" he asks, holding up the flowers.

I swallow. It's really happening. "They're great."

"All right, I'm going to head to the back so I'm not spotted." He grins. "You need to calm down, or you're going to give it away the minute she sees you."

I roll my eyes as Brant and Daniel cackle beside me. "Thanks for the advice."

Heath shrugs and walks away.

I'm nervous. My palms are sweating, and I'm pretty sure Brant and Daniel can hear my heartbeat from where they stand beside me. I look at my phone again.

"Don't worry," Brant says, clapping me on the shoulder. "They'll get her here."

I sigh. "I know. I just don't want anything to go wrong."

Daniel grins. "Who knew you'd be the biggest mess of us all?"

I suddenly regret teasing him about asking Reese out when I realized he liked her at Brant's wedding. Seems he's got the memory of an elephant.

"There they are." Brant waves his arm in the air, catching Morgan's eye. She grins and starts guiding the women in our direction.

"Evan," Karlee says, surprise evident on her face. "I didn't expect you guys to be here." She looks around. "Where are the kids?"

Brant shrugs. "Susan and Sam had some free time on their hands. They offered to take them for a while. Even the baby."

I was surprised when Brant told me Morgan had agreed to leave Levi for a few hours. After the rough birth experience they'd had, I wasn't sure she'd ever leave his side. He'd been born with the cord wrapped around his neck. For a minute there, they thought he wasn't going to make it.

"Oh," Karlee says, looking at Morgan and Reese. "Did you guys know they were leaving the kids and joining us?"

Reese and Morgan share a look and then nod.

"You DID!" Karlee accuses. "Why didn't you tell me?"

I step forward and take her hand. "It was a surprise, sunshine."

She looks at me, her brows drawn in confusion. "A surprise? Why?"

I shrug, hoping my nerves don't give me away. "For fun," I say. "Life doesn't have enough surprises, I think." I wink at her.

"First stop, funnel cake," Karlee says, taking my hand and pulling me in the direction of the first little stand we see. We order several cakes to share, and wander through the midway looking at the ride options.

"I'd like to check out the craft display," Reese says to the women. "Do you guys mind tagging along?"

Brant, Daniel and I follow behind them, waiting for just the right time to head to the Ferris wheel. By the time the ladies have looked at homemade baskets, quilts, and other craft items, it's time.

"Shall we?" Daniel asks, linking Reese's arm through his elbow. "The sun's about to set, so we should start heading out."

"Wait," Karlee says, looking at all of us. "Can't we at least ride one ride before we go?"

Everyone makes a show of agreeing to one ride, and I let out a relieved sigh.

"Let's go check out the Ferris wheel," I suggest. "I've never been on it when the sun is going down. I bet it's a great view with all the colorful trees and the sunset."

Daniel and Brant agree, of course, and we all head toward the area where the Ferris Wheel stands. I resist the urge to check my phone to make sure everyone else is in place.

As we get closer, Karlee spots Heath standing off to the side. "Hey, Heath's here too," she says waving at him.

He pretends not to notice her until we get closer.

"Heath!" Karlee calls.

He looks in our direction and waves, one hand hidden behind his back. "Oh, hey," he says, smiling at her. "I didn't expect to see you here."

I grin and give him a thumbs up behind her back.

"It was going to be a girls day, but the guys found a sitter and decided to join us." She points over her shoulder. "What are you doing here?"

"Oh," he says. A panicked look crosses his face so fast I wonder if she noticed. "I was hoping to bump into this girl I know," he says lamely.

"Oh, have you found her?" Karlee asks, looking around.

"No, not yet. I'm sure I'll run into her, though."

She nods. "Well, you're welcome to join us."

"Nah, I'm going to keep moving and see if I can find her. I need to leave soon and make sure Mom gets her evening medicine."

Thankfully, Heath's mom is still holding on. She's been cancer-free for the last few scans, and they are hopeful it stays that way. Now she's on some kind of maintenance medicine.

I glance behind me to the lemonade stand where our families are supposed to be waiting to greet us as we come off the ride. I don't see anyone, but that's probably a good thing.

"Better get in line," I tell her. We get behind the one other couple waiting for their turn.

Karlee wraps her arm around my waist. "You know, I was looking forward to a girls' night," she says, glancing up at me.

"Oh," I say, suddenly questioning if this was the best plan.

"But this is even better." She lays her head on my shoulder and I let out a ragged breath.

The ride operator opens the chain and helps the couple in front of us into their car. Heath steps beside me and passes me the bouquet of gerbera daisies he's been hiding behind his back. "Good luck," he whispers.

The operator motions to us, and Karlee leads the way onto the platform and into our car, sliding over to the far side. When the door closes, I clear my throat and hold out the flowers.

"Oh my," Karlee says, looking at the arrangement in my hand. "Where did you get those?" she asks, glancing back at Heath, who's wearing a big grin on his face.

"Oh," she says, bringing the bouquet to her nose. "You really planned this out, didn't you?"

I nod, unable to form words just yet. I wait until the wheel is loaded and starts to turn before reaching into my pocket and pulling out the engagement ring that was my grandmother's. As we reach the top, the wheel stops again. Karlee glances in my direction and gasps.

"Karlee Marie Richards," I say, holding out the ring. "Every day for the last year, I've wanted to ask you to marry me."

She clutches the flowers close to her chest and gasps.

"I knew it was too soon, so I waited. I've enjoyed our adventures, our early dinners before you go to work, our movie marathons on your weekends off. I can't imagine spending another day without asking you this question."

She nods, tears falling from her watery eyes.

"Would you do me the honor of being my wife, my partner, my best friend and co-adventurer to the end of our days?"

I wait, holding my breath for what seems like an eternity before Karlee holds out her left hand and says the one word I've been waiting a year to hear.

"Yes!"

I slide the ring onto her finger and kiss her hand. "She said yes!" I yell over the side. Cheers go up from all the cars on the wheel, and Karlee leans in and presses a kiss to my lips.

"It's gorgeous, Evan." She looks at the ring, and back to the view of the sun setting over the vibrant orange and yellow tree tops. "This is amazing. You're amazing."

"I'm glad you are happy," I say, placing my arm around her shoulders.

We spend the rest of the ride holding each other close and looking out over the treetops as we make our way up and around. She keeps sneaking peeks at the ring on her finger and smiling. I grin each time she does it. I'm so in love with this woman.

The ride slows, and people start to unload. I look for her family and see they are waiting with Heath at the exit. Mom and Dad are there too. The only people missing are Tracey and Lawrence, and they're always late.

We step off the ride, and her sister rushes to her, pulling her into a huge hug. "Oh my gosh, Karlee," she says, holding up Karlee's hand to inspect the ring. "It's beautiful."

Her mom hugs her next, and Karlee mouths "perfect" to me over her shoulder.

I wink and stand back, letting them have this moment.

"Way to show me up," Scott says, stepping closer to my side. "I proposed at a restaurant."

I laugh and glance in his direction, and see he's smiling.

"I'm sure it was perfect for you two," Reese says diplomatically.

"Congratulations, man," Scott says. Keeley waves him over, and he steps away to join her.

"Where did you find such a beautiful ring?" Mrs. Richards asks.

"It was my mom's," Dad says, stepping into the fray holding Mom's hand.

Karlee squeals when my mom pulls her into a hug. "Welcome to the family."

I laugh when Tracey and Lawrence come running up. "We're late, aren't we?" Tracey asks, looking around.

I shrug and give her a hug. "It's fine, Trace."

She makes her way through the group surrounding Karlee and gives her a hug.

"Are you ready for this?" Brant asks, standing back from the fray a bit.

I nod. "I've never been more sure about anything in my life."

Finally, Karlee makes her way back to me and wraps her arms around my neck. "You're surprising," she says. "In the best way."

"I'm so glad you think so."

We spend the next hour talking to our family and friends, and sharing laughs under the tent set up by the stage. There's a live band playing, keeping the atmosphere light. When they switch to a slow song, I glance at Karlee and grin.

Standing, I reach for her. "Dance with me?" I ask. "Please."

She smiles and takes my hand, letting me lead her to the dance floor. As we sway to the soft melody of the love song, I can't help but remember her in my arms at her sister's wedding.

"You know," I say, spinning her around. "If you hadn't needed a date for Keeley's wedding, I may never have found the nerve to ask you out."

She looks up at me from below her lashes. "I think we would have gotten there, eventually."

She lays her head on my shoulder as we move together until the last notes of the song drift away. I lean in and kiss her softly. "Ready for the next part?" I ask, whispering in her ear.

She looks at me and smiles. "With you? Always."

I hope you enjoyed Wishing for the Girl Next Door. I'd love it if you would consider leaving a review on Amazon, Goodreads, or BookBub. Even an "I liked it" is perfect!

Read Heath and Gabby's second chance romance today: http://tinyurl.com/SoldiersWish

If you like Piney Brook, be sure to check out *Bean Wishing for a Latte Love*. A sweet rom-com featuring Lacey, the blue-haired barista, and the new to town Dr. Knox Sullivan. https://tinyurl.com/BeanWishingAvailable on Amazon and included in Kindle Unlimited.

Want to start at the beginning of the series? Read *His Christmas Wish*

Join my newsletter and get a printable bookmark and a who's who in Piney Brook FREE!

https://tinyurl.com/WFTGNDBonus

Also By Tia Marlee

Piney Brook Wishes Series

His Christmas Wish

Sweet Summertime Wishes

Wishing for the Girl Next Door

A Soldier's Wish

The Coffee Loft Series

Bean Wishing for a Latte Love

You Mocha Me Crazy

Let's stay in touch

You can sign up for my newsletter and recieve bonus content reserved for subscribers. Be the first to know about events, new releases, and more. https://tiamarleeauthor.com

Follow me:

BookBub: https://tinyurl.com/BBTiaMarlee

Amazon: https://tinyurl.com/AmazonTiaMarlee

Goodreads: https://tinyurl.com/GRTiaMarlee

Facebook: https://tinyurl.com/FBTiaMarlee

Instagram: https://tinyurl.com/IGTiaMarlee

Website: https://tiamarlee.com

Join my Facebook group: https://tinyurl.com/TiaMarleeReader Group

About the Author

Tia Marlee resides in Central Texas with her husband and three teenaged children. When she isn't writing, Tia enjoys reading, embroidery and spending time with her family. Tia is the author of the Piney Book Wishes series featuring unexpected love stories based in small-town Piney Brook, Arkansas.

Printed in Great Britain
by Amazon